JUL 17 2019

NO LONGER PROPERTY OF
SEATTLE PUBLIC LIBRARY

D0962472

The
BOBCAT

A NOVEL

KATHERINE FORBES RILEY

Arcade Publishing • New York

Copyright © 2019 by Katherine Forbes Riley

All rights reserved. No part of this book may be reproduced in any manner without the express written consent of the publisher, except in the case of brief excerpts in critical reviews or articles. All inquiries should be addressed to Arcade Publishing, 307 West 36th Street, 11th Floor, New York, NY 10018.

Arcade Publishing books may be purchased in bulk at special discounts for sales promotion, corporate gifts, fund-raising, or educational purposes. Special editions can also be created to specifications. For details, contact the Special Sales Department, Arcade Publishing, 307 West 36th Street, 11th Floor, New York, NY 10018 or arcade@skyhorsepublishing.com.

Arcade Publishing® is a registered trademark of Skyhorse Publishing, Inc.®, a Delaware corporation.

Visit our website at www.arcadepub.com.

10 9 8 7 6 5 4 3 2 1

Library of Congress Cataloging-in-Publication Data is available on file.

Print ISBN: 978-1-94892-409-2
Ebook ISBN: 978-1-94892-411-5

Printed in the United States of America

For Enrico, Alexander, and Etienne

A picture held us captive, and we could not seem to get outside of it. For it lay in our language and our language seemed to repeat it to us inexorably.

~ Ludwig Wittgenstein

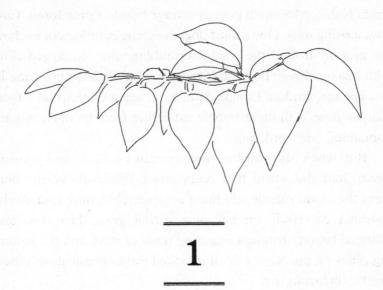

1

Physically the fog signaled only the tail end of a long Vermont winter. But nature assumed a kind of sentience, given space. So it pillowed against Laurelie's windows as a soft asylum wall and leaked its internal fluids on the sills and acted as a deranged refractor on the view, magnifying the crags and pores down her cottage's stone walls into dizzying cliffs, while drowning the yard and forest beyond in uniform gray particulate.

Laurelie sat for a while with her forehead pressed to the screen, imagining what it would feel like if she'd woken to a dawn in which there really was no one else left. Then she got down on the floor and pulled her body through its stretches while sketching the panels for *Apocalypse* in her head, each image carefully and almost playfully brutal, modeling them after

Frida Kahlo. Mountain pose, a cottage beside a pine forest. Cat-cow, a rising mist. Downward dog, the scene panning out to show the ground around the cottage crumbling away to jagged cliffs with black oblivion beyond. Pigeon pose, a shadow appearing in one cottage window. Lunge, panning in again to focus on a face. Corpse pose, a thought bubble extending from its open mouth, containing one word: *Safe*.

But when she finished her exercises and looked outside again, half the world had reappeared. While above the lilac trees the cloud mantle still hung impenetrable, now spiderwebs sparkled cheerfully on her new spring grass. Her dirt lane plunged bravely through lingering trails of mist, and the towering pines on the other side of it looked rather comical with their heads still lost in fog.

Suddenly, a blur of motion, a change of light—something threaded through their trunks. Instantly she stepped back and pressed her body to the wall beside the window. Her heart flailed like a bird in her chest, trapped by her own rapid shallow breaths, as she searched the gloomy understory for further signs of life. The fog light heightened contrasts, turning the trunks dark and the low growth bright, and the air between them almost blue. But though she remained there watching for a long time, nothing else moved.

Later she rode her bike down the dirt lane to where it met the river road. There, ice computed a massive geometry, drifting white in shards down the new black water that came and went to her right through the trees. Woods lined the first half of this stretch of the road, which followed the arc of the river east for two miles or so before both turned southward. Above her birds swooped and perched, their clamor swelling and subsiding with her breath. When she emerged from the forest, fog-dampened and winded, the sky showed blue patches like puzzle pieces. The sun laid a warm hand on her back. She basked a little, letting the road's slow torque carry her along a meadow sprouting blue-bells and snowdrops and the occasional surprised tulip. Forested hills undulated beyond it all the way to the horizon where rose, still obscured by cloud, the silhouettes of mountains.

Then came a sharp bend, where the road followed the river south, and she turned left and headed up a steep hill lined with the beer can–littered yards of Greek fraternity houses, cheap white clapboard structures in various states of disorder and disrepair. She kept her head averted as she climbed but it made little difference. Still she was trembling by the time she reached the top, where the road became High Street and intersected Main Street, the commercial district of Montague, Vermont. Across the intersection lay the campus green of Montague College, the small school that shared the town's name. Encircling the green's far side were the half dozen ivy-covered buildings that constituted the college itself. Even on this warm spring morning they seemed to huddle in, their shoulders hunched against the wilderness crowding in behind them. The scattering of people coming and going looked like ants against the great backdrop of trees. And yet, even as she joined them, Laurelie felt herself apart. Putting on her headphones and casting down her eyes, she felt no more weighted than they but rather like a storm cloud, gathering darkly and unseen as she walked to meet her senior thesis advisor about a series of panels she fervently wished he'd never seen.

She'd started making them after arriving in Montague the

prior fall, following more than a year of not drawing at all. The first set of panels had come to her during a ride to campus one late November morning so cold she'd actually thought she wouldn't make it. Eyes blinded by sun bouncing off two inches of freshly plowed snow, lungs so frozen they could hardly expand, she'd stopped feeling her fingers halfway there and had to hope they'd stay wrapped around her handlebars. Upon cresting the hill into town, she'd stumbled into the first door she found open and received its jangle of bells and heated rush of air like life returning. It was a little shop on High Street tucked in the corner of the little alley that ran along behind Main and turned out to be the local general store. Full of cramped overflowing aisles that sold everything imaginable and more, it also had an old machine that spat hot drinks and half a dozen scarred school desks pushed up against the windows on its side wall. From the corner desk she could see the post office and the backs of other shops across the alley, as well as a slice of intersection and the green beyond. On that frozen morning it had seemed that everyone but her knew to stay inside, for she had sat drinking cups of sweet hot chocolate and nursing her fingers and ears for almost an hour before anyone else came into view through the murky diamonds of the lead-pane windows. The woman she finally saw was old and frail and covered in black from head to foot. Laurelie watched her cross the empty street and then climb the post office stairs, and after a while the scene began to feel so much like a slowly changing still life that she had taken out her sketchpad to try to capture it. There were twenty stairs and the old woman had paused a full minute between each one, maybe taking care with her footing or maybe just catching her breath, but either way not holding onto the railing and never, ever looking up. Afterward, the panels had reminded Laurelie of *Whistler's*

Mother, done as they were all in gray and black, composed of only a few simple shapes, the square framing wall of the building behind her, the sharp-edged stairs, and the pronounced curve of the old woman's body. She'd arranged the panels in a sequence to show the woman's slow progress up the stairs, like a comic strip except not funny at all. Later she'd added thought bubbles extending from the woman's head. The one on the bottom step reflected a buxom young maiden, who then slowly morphed through each panel into a careworn matron on the middle stair, and at the top became the old crone herself, except far older, impossibly ancient, her face etched with her journey's pain.

After that Laurelie had started going to the general store every morning. Sometimes the bell would jingle as a customer came in, but at that early hour no one else sat at the windows. There was only one clerk and she sat and read magazines up at the register; it felt like Laurelie was the only one there. She'd down cups of hot chocolate while looking out the window, waiting for the urge to draw to return. The Montague students and professors who passed her corner view never sparked it, and neither did the hippies or Appalachian Trail hikers who were legion in Montague, flashing dreadlocks and tattoos like nonconformity beacons. The second time it didn't even come from outside. It was a kid hunched over a laptop inside the general store. No older than twelve or thirteen, he should have been in school, at his own desk, not hers. She was about to turn around and leave when he looked up at her and scowled. More than an expression, it was an illumination, exposing the general size and shape of his pain. She sat behind him then, at the very last desk and spent the rest of the morning trying to capture it. She modeled these panels after Caravaggio's *Narcissus* and again used the comic strip format, with his body in each panel leaning a little closer to a screen in which only his own reflection appeared. Everything else was black except for those twin faces, and the thought bubbles coming from their angry mouths were filled with tiny statements of computer code.

The last set of panels she'd only just completed. They depicted a man she'd seen slumped against the wall of the little pub next door to the general store on her way in one day. After a week of warm weather no one was wearing a coat anymore, but he was still bundled in heavy winter outerwear. Some of it had looked military, and his face was heavily bearded, and the lines of his hands were embedded with dirt. As she'd ridden past she'd imagined him trapped somewhere so deep inside himself that he couldn't feel the heat. His panels she'd based on Picasso's *Guernica*, the scene a picturesque town but its streets as he walked them littered with images of violence only he could see, a woman on a corner grieving over a dead infant, a severed hand in a gutter, a figure in a doorway entrapped by fire, and the thought bubbles coming from his head were filled with "Pows!" and "Whams!" and his own screams.

For half a year she'd worked on these panels in isolation, and now, pulling open the Studio Art Department door, she felt the vulnerability of an animal emerging weak after long hibernation, a feeling that only intensified when she encountered her advisor standing in the entryway collecting his mail. She thought he resembled some small predator, stocky and hairy with shoulders that sloped precipitously and a belly that pouched like a laundry bag over heavily muscled legs. He greeted her, she imagined, rapaciously, showing all his small teeth and the dark wet space behind them as he held his office door open for her. The room was like him, small and overstuffed; in addition to his own desk he'd fit a large pillowy couch on one side of a coffee table and squeezed in two wooden chairs on the other.

She sat down on one of the chairs and he settled onto the couch, whistling "Oh, What a Beautiful Mornin'." He always chose the couch and so she always chose a chair, because the one time she hadn't she'd smelled his meat breath and flinched every time he moved and couldn't process a single word he said. He soon stopped whistling but the words of the song continued looping in her head while he sat looking at her across the table and she sat looking down at her hands. Meanwhile something high and finely tuned was gathering force inside her, rising in both volume and pitch until it filled her throat and she was sure she would choke.

"The lilacs are budding," she blurted. And then, leaning over so that her hair hid her face, she rummaged through her backpack, first for her pen and then for her notebook and finally for nothing at all except to keep her body folded over her knees. The word "budding" had done it, she realized too late, and her horror at having uttered it was only magnified by the fact that it was true: now near the end of April, the leggy trees that grew like weeds all over Montague were sprouting hard green protrusions all up and down their branches.

Hearing pages rustle, she looked up. Her advisor had the manila folder she'd left in his mailbox spread open on the coffee table and was riffling through her pages. *The Truant* flashed past, suicide-eyed, and then the tired body of *The Crone*. Reaching the last page, her advisor sat back again, leaving the mad grimace of *The Veteran* exposed.

"Well, there certainly is a lot of effort here," he said.

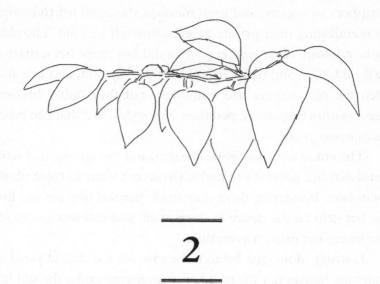

2

She rode down the hill wishing the fog would return, so that the sky did not feel so exposed. Her advisor had spent the whole meeting posing questions to her that felt like attacks, although he had assured her they were only hypothetical, their greater significance something for her to ponder as she developed her ideas for her senior thesis. But they were questions too bureaucratic to ever have a clear answer. Like, what did she intend to convey through her "high art" references? And was her use of "low art" techniques meant to disarm the high art references and make them less intimidating? What if instead they were seen as demeaning, or even defacing the old masters' artistry? He had wondered, moreover, what motivated her choices of subject matter, and why she had chosen to only represent people at the periphery of society, and what message she intended to convey by manifesting their private agonies through cartoon. The ability to replicate other masters' styles did not make her a master, he'd said. Copying was a useful learning method, and one that even the old masters had employed, but they didn't become masters until they developed their own styles, and that had taken them many years.

The entire hour had gone like that, and though she had written down her advisor's remarks, she didn't want to think about them later. Pondering them only made her feel like she was losing her grip on the desire to draw at all, and this was too much like losing her grip on everything.

Leaving Montague behind, she saw not the dismal yards of fraternity houses nor the meadow shimmering under the sun nor the slow curve of the river road around it, but rather a crowded Philadelphia street and her own form walking along it with her headphones on and her head down. Whenever this particular image filled her mind and panic climbed inside, she would immediately superimpose another one upon it, one of herself boarding the Greyhound bus that had carried her away from those streets the previous fall. In her mind she again watched more cities come and go through the bus windows as it brought her north, until all signs of civilization faded away and only wilderness remained, fractured by a single stripe of road and countless evergreens, all those hundreds of thousands of trees seeming to stand sentry, bounding and guarding her escape.

After parking her bike at her cottage, she climbed the hill to the main house. There she found the little boy she babysat each afternoon kneeling in the grass, pushing around his yellow construction trucks with his head bent low to watch their wheels, soft growling sounds escaping his lips. She bent and ruffled his golden hair, and when he raised his arms to her she lifted him onto her hip and whispered hello into his ear.

The boy's mother was standing a few yards away, looking down at an easel and frowning. She wore an immaculate white smock over a pale linen dress and a wide-brimmed white sunhat perched atop the polished waves of her gray-gold bob. In the winter when Laurelie had come to pick up her son she'd be freshly groomed and on her way out, but since the weather had warmed she had started taking a class on landscape painting. The teacher, she'd confided to Laurelie, was a hunk, and most afternoons now when Laurelie arrived she was outside practicing her technique. Currently she was painting three hills in the distance. With their new spring foliage Laurelie saw them as softly feminine, the curves of a woman reclining in a fuzzy green gown, but her landlady's use of thick impasto made them threats, hunkering dark and brutish at the horizon.

"Be sure to have him home by six," the woman said, dabbing critically at a feather of cloud. "He'll need to be bathed and dressed. You always bring him home so dirty, and we're having guests tonight."

Laurelie nodded, already moving off down the hill. The boy in her arms began to wriggle, anticipating what came next. As soon as they were out of sight of the house, she put him down and took his hand, and together they began to run.

After nearly eight months in Montague, Laurelie's dread of

human contact felt no less visceral than it had back in Philadelphia, but in certain cases she could now force herself to overcome it. Like meeting with her advisor so she could finally finish college, and renting the cottage from the boy's parents so that she did not have to live on campus. Lacking funds to pay the entire rent, she'd had to arrange to babysit their son in partial payment. But she'd never even met her landlord, and although she saw her landlady every afternoon, the woman kept these interactions brief. The boy himself didn't trigger the dread; in fact despite his gender he had the opposite effect. She thought this was because he was only two and a half and possessed so little in the way of personal substance. To him the whole world was new and he knew nothing for certain yet. And when she was with him her own fears loosened their hold, so that curiosity and even pleasure sometimes emerged, as hungry and furtive as the field mice in her cottage's walls.

She and the boy spent most of their time outdoors. His father worked in the upper echelons of Montague College and their manor house sprawled atop a large grassy mound a few miles from the town green. At the bottom of it, tucked away in a corner, sat Laurelie's own cottage, once the servant quarters. The whole parcel of land was surrounded by a hundred miles of forest preserve, and a dirt lane encircled the private land, separating it from the preserve and connecting it to the river road that Laurelie rode each day toward campus. Across the lane and directly opposite her cottage, a trail wound its way down to the river. Since discovering it, she and the boy had gone down there nearly every day.

Always, however, they stopped at her cottage first, for he delighted in visiting her cats. Running with her down the hill he'd already be shouting "Caa!" into the wind he made. She gave him treats to use to win them over, and he squeaked with pleasure while the boy cat purred and licked them from his fingers. Then he ran upstairs clutching more treats in his moist fist and pushed them back as far as he could into the dark space underneath Laurelie's bed, where the girl cat ran to hide whenever she heard him coming.

Task accomplished, they crossed the dirt lane and headed down the river trail. No wider than the height of the boy, it measured less than a quarter mile in length, but still they could lose an hour along the way. Today the boy was taking his time collecting treasures, stuffing his pockets full of stones while Laurelie carried the rest in a sack she made from the bottom of her T-shirt. But as soon as he heard the river's chuckle he began to trot, and when the trail gave way to a root-threaded bank, he danced impatiently while she removed their shoes.

They stepped together into the water. "Cold," she murmured, but he didn't answer, too intent on his study of his feet. The water was so clear they could see every grain of the fine black mud their entrance had puffed up from the river floor. Again and again he wiggled his toes, and then after a while he raised his head and they headed further in, but still the water reached no higher than his knees by the time they reached their destination.

Thinking Rock jutted out of the river ten feet from shore, perfectly flat and glittering darkly, the air above it sparkling as particle-filled rays of sunlight filtered down through the canopy. She lifted the boy up first and then clambered after him, and they sat with their backs in the direction they'd come, looking out over another twenty feet of water stretching away on the other side. The rock must have marked a hidden chasm, for it seemed another river entirely here, this one deep and fast and wide. Every time they came its color varied, as did its flow. During the winter it had ranged through every shade of black, sometimes glossy and others dull, its edges frozen and piled with snow, while the middle still pulsed its thick life's blood. But as spring took hold it had lightened and thinned; the last time they'd come it had looked like chocolate milk.

"Gee," the boy pronounced, and then with a hint of cere-mony, began removing stones from his pockets. Laurelie unrolled her shirt and handed over the items within, one yellow forsythia branch, one dead orange and black caterpillar, one smooth stick bare of bark, one drooping cluster of bluebells, and one still-crisp white narcissus. All of these he carefully arranged according to some private order, shifting and reorganizing the whole lot often to accommodate each new piece. While he worked she leaned back with her legs dangling down over the side of the rock, barely brushing the water, and considered its color herself. The boy was right; there was green inside the brown today, she decided, a deep lustrous olive.

"Buh." He'd been turning a smooth gray rock in his hands, and now dropped it into the deep side of the river.

"Yes, it did bubble," she affirmed, "when it sank. Which one of your treasures won't sink, do you think?"

After considering the question awhile, he threw in the for-sythia branch, and together they watched it float away, seeming at times to struggle and others to tease as it swirled into eddies and snagged on roots but always worked its way free.

Once the boy had given all his treasures to the river, she fished a granola bar from her pocket and they shared it. The sound of their crunching merged with the river's low burble and the forest's stillness, which seemed to have a sound all its own. In her head she was sketching it, soft and full of light with the trees reflecting back the color of the sky in the style of Monet, when a squirrel rattled a warning high in a tree. Abruptly the scene twisted, turning hellish, hedonistic, as the squirrel continued rattling and the boy clutched her shoulders, crying, "Caa!" over and over until she too turned to see.

At first there was only the forest. The riverbank, trees, river, and the trail from which they'd come. Then a shape she'd taken for shade detached itself from a large growth of ferns off to her left. Slowly, it approached.

The boy was right. It was a cat. Although this one was three times larger than her own boy cat, at least. It had a tan coat with black striping that hung loose down its legs and then fluted out into a ruff of a lighter hue around its neck. Its ears were large and black and tufted, and its tail was just a stump. Silently it padded to the water's edge, and then stopped and bent its head. Its tongue emerged and began lapping at the water, slowly, dreamlike, the pink flesh shedding fat droplets from both edges that sparkled as they fell, full of sunlight.

"Paa?"

"Hush," she said to the boy and squeezed him, for the large cat had frozen when he spoke, and was now staring directly at them.

She herself had no urge to pet it. Even the idea made her lose her breath. The cat was stunning, but in her mind's eye each element of its beauty equally signaled threat. Its eyes and ears and nose and mouth appeared to her like giant receptors, constantly seeking prey. Its rear legs were thickly muscled, and disproportionately longer than its front ones, built for catching prey. Its four large paws looked soft and puffy but they bore strong curved claws sheathed beneath, precisely spaced to hold and puncture prey. Now that it had finished drinking, she thought it would surely leave, but instead it sat back on its haunches and cleaned first its face and then its ruff. And then, when it finished its ablutions, it just sat there, staring off at the trees as if it had forgotten all about them. But one of its ears was still aimed in their direction, and it twitched with every movement she or the boy made. The longer this dissemblance went on the greater her anxiety about it became, until finally she forced her gaze away. Beyond it the trail beckoned, promising safety, but the cat sat too close, barely a foot to its left. Looking behind her, she gauged the distance to the opposite shore. Nothing had changed. It was still too far and cold and deep to swim with a two-and-a-half-year-old boy.

"Paa-Paa-Paa-Paa-Paa—"

She swiveled back fast, half-bracing to jump, and saw a second form emerge from the trees. This one was human, and male. Panic swamped her and then slowly dissipated as she took in the boots he wore and the pack on his back, for he was surely an AT hiker, and a lost one at that. The Appalachian Trail threaded through this forest preserve a few miles from where she sat. As he got closer she observed more of the details of him, how tall he was and how thin, the depth of color of his exposed skin, but because he was looking down at the ground all she saw was a wild mass of dark hair.

Had he even noticed the cat? For that matter, had it noticed him? It still hadn't moved, beyond the single flick of an ear. But even as she was wondering what to do, the hiker looked up. She only saw his face for a moment before he returned his gaze to the ground, but it was enough to register his lack of surprise as he surveyed the scene, and she took this as an indication that he'd already processed it.

Head down again, he proceeded to the river and there

crouched behind the cat, who for its part stretched languorously and then turned and bumped its head against his knee. The boy could barely contain himself as the hiker trailed a slow hand down its back. Laurelie, however, now observing the cat from the side, was shocked by how swollen its belly was, distended so far it nearly touched the ground.

The hiker was gazing at the cat, who was gazing back at him. His eyes were long and wide-set above sharply jutting cheekbones, and his mouth was broad and slightly pointed at its edges above a triangular chin, so that looking back and forth between them, Laurelie thought he and the cat shared a kind of family resemblance.

Then, as she watched, his eyes filled with tears, and one spilled over, tracking luminescent down his russet skin.

Flushing hot, Laurelie looked down at the rock, at her pale knobby feet, at her dirty T-shirt smeared with pollen and pine sap. He wasn't actually crying, she told herself, and yet the boy in her arms seemed to think so as well, for already his face was bunching up in sympathy. Hearing him whimper, her own fear swelled. Gripping him tightly, she slid down off the rock and began sloshing away through the shallow water, intending to give both cat and hiker a wide berth before heading for shore.

But the boy cried out, "Daa!" He wanted down. They struggled for a few steps, each one's distress only escalating the other's until finally she gave in. The moment his feet touched water he calmed, grew placid even as she hurried him along, telling herself the cat wasn't following even as she imagined on her back the grip and tear of its claws.

Reaching the riverbank, she cut straight through the brush for some yards before heading back toward the trail, so that when they did break onto it they were already a few yards along.

She stopped then, they both did, their heads turning in unison to locate the intruders once more.

If they hadn't looked at just that moment they would have missed the cat, for it was loping back toward the ferns from which it had come. Laurelie's relief at seeing the threat reduced by half faded as she watched the cat move away. At that distance its beauty overwhelmed its risk, but also conveyed clearly that something was wrong. For one step of every four was out of rhythm with the rest. The cat was limping—badly.

The boy had lost interest in the cat. He'd spied their shoes at the head of the trail and was trotting back for them. "No!" Laurelie said, reaching out to stop him. When her hand closed on air she gasped and hurried after him.

Already he was sitting down, preparing for her to put his shoes on. But his attention was fixed on the hiker, still crouched by the water's edge, who had turned away now, and was gazing after the cat. Distantly, she thought, *he looks like a dropped marionette, with those long thin legs folded and the arms and shoulders arcing over them.* The corners of his mouth were pointing down and the space between his brows was deeply furrowed. He looked worried, she realized, and in the next instant, she said, "I think its leg's hurt," startling herself as much as him.

He rose then, all jostling towering limbs, swamping her again with the peril of him. She took an involuntary step back. But now he froze, just like the cat, and stood there looking off at the ferns from which they'd come. No ear swiveled, but still she sensed a kind of invisible field around him, trembling, listening. His hands were pushed deep into the front pockets of his pants, claws sheathed. She could hear his breath coming fast and shallow, saw his mouth was open and his nostrils were flared, pushing at their skin so hard the edges had gone white.

"A hunter shot her," he said, and then after a moment, answering her unspoken question, added, "Not here. Up near Bangor, on Barren Mountain."

Bangor, Maine. That was three hundred miles north. She wondered how they'd gotten here and decided they must have walked.

"She can't hunt, so she won't den. Just keeps running." A ripple traveled over his shoulders then. "Kittens'll be coming soon," he said.

"Caa," said the boy. She looked down at him. Next to him on the forest floor was a pile of tight green pine cones. He was opening and closing his hands and regarding them with an intent expression. In the same instant she realized they were covered in sap, he put them on his cheeks, first one, and then the other. He smiled at this, until he tried to pull them off again. She sank down then and gently peeled them free, and wiped them off as best she could with her T-shirt.

When she looked up again, the hiker was gone.

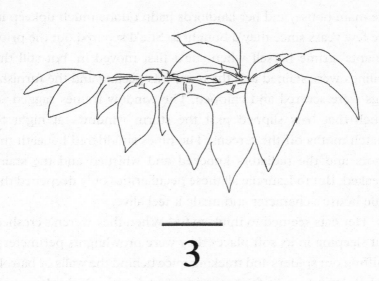

3

After dropping the boy at home she walked back down the hill alone. It was six o'clock already but the sun was still high; this late in April and so far north it would not set for hours yet. From a distance, dappled in warm light and framed by woods, her cottage looked like a fairy's house, pulsating with energy and motion, an impression that remained as she got closer, for its perspective hardly changed. Small and square, the cottage had only a few rooms, a kitchen and living room downstairs, and a bedroom and bathroom upstairs. But those rooms were spacious and full of light, and outside there was a large front porch and a yard that bathed in sun all day and was bordered by lilacs and sugar maples. Still, the cottage was over a century old, and it showed its age. Long ago it had been the servants' quarters for the main house, and her landlords hadn't done much upkeep in the few years since they'd bought it. She'd scoured out the prior tenants' grime herself when she'd first moved in, but still the ceilings were stained and the paint was peeling and the furnishings were scarred and chipped. The window frames sagged so much that bats slipped past the storm windows at night to snatch moths off the screens. The pipes shuddered beneath the floors and the radiators knocked and whistled and the stairs creaked. But to Laurelie all these peculiarities only deepened the little house's character and made it feel alive.

Her cats seemed to think so too. When they weren't crashed out sleeping in its soft places they were prowling its perimeters, sniffing out spiders and tracking mice behind the walls or patrolling the windowsills for bats and the red squirrels that ran their circuits along the house's foundation. They guarded against her own ghosts as well; whenever the atmosphere grew somber or anxious, first one cat and then the other would spontaneously tear through the room, ears cocked and eyes wild, claws skittering for purchase as they chased invisibles across the old wideboard floors.

They were indoor cats; she never let them out, not since finding them the prior spring abandoned in a Philadelphia park. At the time she'd thought an urban environment contained too many threats to them, and now she thought the same about a rural one. Bobcats, for one! She could hardly believe she'd encountered an actual bobcat only a few hours before, and less than a quarter mile from her cottage. Preparing herself a simple dinner of fruit and bread and cheese, she imagined it stalking the birds in her yard, clawing the bark of her sugar maples, hiding in the grass and then springing, trapping a beating pulse between its teeth and gently squeezing until the blood burst. She stopped then, not letting herself consider what it would do to her own cats. Thankfully they seemed content to remain indoors. Even now with the windows wide and the spring evening pouring in sounds and colors and scents, they were lolling on their backs with their heads together, cleaning their ruffs in the blocks of light stacked across her living room floor.

She, however, was feeling restless, and so took herself outside to eat her meal on the front porch. Sitting on the top step, she looked out at the sun inching down through the pines, illuminating every detail of their outer branches without ever penetrating the secrets they hid inside. Including the bobcat the hiker had been following for three hundred miles. It must have taken weeks. She tried to imagine how it must have felt to be immersed in every wild detail of spring as it pushed itself up through dying winter. What, she wondered, munching her own food, did they eat? He'd said the bobcat couldn't hunt. She imagined him foraging for wild mushrooms, nuts and berries, perhaps even trapping small animals for it, and then pushed the rest of that thought away and considered instead where they might sleep, and whether they traveled by day or night, and how he could have kept up with a wild animal, even a wounded one.

The journey seemed impossible. But then so did the fact that it had led them to her front door. And didn't every journey seem impossible at first? Sharp and sticking, the truth remained that without a map, without a finger tracing along a path, there could be no certainty as to where one might end up. She thought of her first days back in Philadelphia. Who would have known that path would lead here? She thought of her freshman dorm room, the complete opposite of the sunny cottage in which she now resided. She remembered being so relieved to have been allotted a single, and how the feeling had dissipated, trickling away in slow leaks as she took in the space, for it had been so small and dim, with only one lamp and no overhead light and a window that looked out at a brick wall. And waiting behind that leaking relief had been the realization that the ugly little room contained the sum total of all that was now hers. It was this she kept thinking about long after her father and stepmother had backed out the door with awkward waves. She'd sat on her new bed eyeing her door and had been unable to come up with a good enough reason to leave until finally her bladder forced the situation. Then she'd walked the long hall to the bathroom and taken the longest pee of her life.

She'd been washing her hands while avoiding the mirror, too afraid of what she might see there, when the door opened.

Much later Laurelie would sketch this scene, the doll-like creature sauntering in, cocking her hip with a hand on it and saying, "I *saw* you moving in. You're the *only* cool person in this *entire* dorm. You *must* be from The City too."

What city? Laurelie had thought at the time. The girl hadn't seemed real, so tiny and porcelain-skinned, with long chestnut curls spilling down her back and a torso long and flat as a boy's beneath a lacy blouse tucked into tight jeans, shiny leather boots encasing her legs to the knees. Despite her small stature she commanded attention as she moved across the floor. Laurelie couldn't remember exactly what else she'd said but could recall with near-perfect crystalline sequencing how she'd sashayed to the mirror and pursed her lips, then lifted her chin and examined both profiles, and finally sprung her curls and, with a sway of her miniature hips, turned to inspect the view from behind.

The memory made Laurelie shudder now, but then all her memories of Philadelphia did, all of them imbued with the same sick dread, possessed of a menace they'd hardly suggested at the time. In fact the girl had invited Laurelie back to her room and she'd felt like a character in a Woody Allen movie sitting on that lacy bed, lacy pillows piled high at her back, listening to the girl talk about "The City."

Over the weeks that followed Laurelie passed many hours in that room, listening to the girl talk about her hometown. It was a place she referred to so often and with such reverence that Laurelie was soon envisioning the phrase lit up in neon lights. The girl would discuss her favorite designers at length, and all the celebrities she'd seen and pretended not to, for this of course was what New Yorkers did, being the most sophisticated people in the world. The girl often took sly shots like this at everyone not from New York, seemed not to even see that they might be insulting, except for when they specifically targeted her roommate, a shy Iowan of large proportions who made her own clothes and admittedly made easy prey for such a rich and fashionable New Yorker. But then everything became her target, including their university and the other students that attended it, not to mention the city of Philadelphia itself. The girl openly despised it as if it intentionally competed with New York, and contemplated having to live there permanently—there or in any another city—with a theatrical shudder. According to her everything that mattered happened in New York or Paris or, occasionally and regrettably, Los Angeles.

And yet for some reason Laurelie could not understand, the doll girl cleaved to her, a native Pittsburgher. As weeks turned to months the girl still insisted they take all their meals together, and study together, and spend their free time going to fraternity parties or else hanging out in her room. Always her room—she hated Laurelie's "cave"—and it was true that her room was brighter and bigger, and better once her roommate learned to stay away. Then little by little she started collecting other girls too, all of them tiny and exactly like her, girls from New York or LA or other select cities who listened to her City stories avidly and sang along to her pop albums and perused her fashion magazines far more enthusiastically than Laurelie. They brought along their own designer clothes and together, with much laughter and fraudulent appraisal, assembled in the hours before each fraternity party close approximations to what they saw in their magazines, while Laurelie watched silently from the bed. Since Laurelie herself owned no designer brands, the doll girl, disparaging of her T-shirts and jeans, would eventually have to compose an ensemble from the stuff of her own closet, none of which fit Laurelie's taller, bustier form.

None of it fit Laurelie. And yet she never resisted. It was as if when she was with them her mind whispered from a great distance. In fact the only time it functioned properly was late at night, alone in her dorm room. She'd come back from frat parties and lie sleepless on her bed, listening to the British rock she'd liked in high school and remembering her pre-college self like the funky thrift-shop coat she'd once worn everywhere and then somehow, somewhere lost. How tough she'd been! How world-wise! Growing up basically on her own, her mother almost never home and wrapped up in her boyfriends on the rare occasions when she was.

Now at college, the only thing about herself that Laurelie still recognized was her art. A hobby at home, it became a necessity as that first winter progressed. She began carrying a sketchbook everywhere and drew all the places she found herself in, letting the action roll out around her as if she weren't a part of it. And then she became the recipient of the other girls' snide barbs as they minced en masse down the lamplit streets of Frat Row.

They never rejected her, not openly; it was more like she drifted to their furthest periphery, where she still swelled their numbers and they could either ignore or disparage her without letting go completely. Meanwhile she was moving so deep inside herself as to hardly care that she'd become a parody to them. She filled notebooks with noir studies of off-key bands and wasted crowds and status-gauging. Wilting in a corner drinking sour beer, she drew her troupe of doll girls blossoming in fetid frat basement air, attracting males not through any natural allure but with the pungency of artificial sensuality that threaded through their voices and gestures. She drew fraternity brothers cruising the rooms with shark faces. Sometimes one of them would effect some violation like nudging her drawing arm or tugging her ponytail, and then, smiling broadly, catalogue the swell of her breasts. All of this she incorporated into her drawings while playing no active role in those scenes at all, until one night at a spring formal afterparty near the end of her freshman year.

Everyone was still dressed for the runway, but coming apart now at the seams. Laurelie sat sketching the bow ties discarded on the tables, the high heels scattered underneath. A fraternity brother passing by saw the empty beer cup at her elbow and offered to get her a refill. She'd hardly noticed it empty, and now hardly noticed it full, nor the brother who lingered as she drank once, maybe twice from the new cup before the china marker fell from her hand. Her body flooded hot and then cold. Her vision blurred and when she stood she was swept by nausea and would have fallen if the fraternity brother hadn't caught her.

After that there were only flashes of memory. Endless hallways, endless stairs. Still having thoughts, but her muscles no longer responding. Throwing up somewhere. Voices coming at her from underwater, and someone telling her to lie down, and then her body jolting and shuddering as it was moved around.

She'd woken the next morning in an empty room. It was dawn and the hallway and stairs were deserted, and the only thing she'd felt at first was relief at leaving the place behind. The sunlight was blinding, splashing off the sidewalks as she made her way back to her dorm. Head throbbing as if it'd been struck, she stood under a hot shower until it turned cold while her mind slipped slow vines around the night before, seeking hours she simply couldn't remember. Back in her room she catalogued her bruises, but shied away from any thought of what might be wrong inside, where it ached and burned. She slept and then wrote a term paper, slept again and wrote another one. She studied for her final exams. She stayed in her room, avoiding the other girls, and none of them sought her out. A week later, when her period came, she cried.

Hardly had she gotten home that summer when her mother kicked her out again. She'd gotten remarried while Laurelie was at college and said she didn't like her daughter's new attitude. So Laurelie moved in with her father and stepmother. They worked a lot, and after kicking around their house alone for a week she got a job at a local art store. The pay was terrible but she got free paper, and so mostly when she wasn't working she drew. She copied old masters from the coffee table books in the living room while classical music poured from her father's speakers; she could no longer stand popular music, anything that might be played at frat parties. Once she went out with some old friends from high school but ended up leaving early; she couldn't bear the smell of beer and all the smiles looked like masks and all the words sounded untrue. By September she couldn't walk without limping, having peeled the skin from her heels in blood-beading divots, and was contemplating dyeing her hair black, or shaving it all off.

It was actually a relief to return to college, to busy her mind with school. She had elected to remain in the same dorm room, because even tiny and dark it was now infinitely preferable to sharing space with a stranger. When she wasn't in class she would hole up there or in the library and draw. She was always either drawing or thinking about it. It helped keep the other images at bay. Flashes of a heavy body pressing down on hers, a few fractured seconds of colors and shapes and scents from that night, distorted and horrifying, yet as vivid as a waking dream. Inside buildings she considered corners and angles, the relative sizes and shapes of objects. Outside, walking between venues, she focused on the views, on the blending shades of the changing leaves and the interactions between temperatures and lights.

She didn't go home that winter, or the following summer either. Instead she got a job in an on-campus kitchen to pay her summer housing fee. She audited a graduate level class in ancient art history. And drifting between those two landscapes, one so far in the past and the other before her eyes, it felt as if nothing were real.

Then the air cooled again, and fall term of her junior year began. One afternoon, walking through a tree-lined campus courtyard, she came upon a couple embracing. Backlit by the burnished autumn hues, his blond head was bent to her dark one, and his body curled down around hers with no light at all between them. It was a scene so picture-perfect that she paused for a second look.

After a year, she'd stopped fearing that she'd accidentally encounter him. She'd convinced herself she wouldn't even recognize him if she did. And then suddenly there it was, that thrusting chin, those pillow cheeks, that smile rising up to smother deep slices of eyes, and once more she lay crushed beneath that chest, tasting that firewater tongue.

Standing there she had felt like she was at the edge of great abyss, like something momentous was about to happen. And then, like a bird sensing currents, the girl had looked over at Laurelie. She was a tiny girl, a porcelain girl. A doll girl in a winter-white coat, a red beret cocked rakishly on her chestnut curls.

She'd looked at Laurelie, and then turned her head and whispered something to the rapist that made him laugh. Both of them had looked at Laurelie then, and laughed.

And Laurelie had simply walked away.

Nothing momentous had occurred, but after that she'd begun crossing streets, using back alleys and fire doors. She'd entered every enclosed space with a nervous heart, everywhere feeling people looking, hearing whispers and laughter as if they were directed at her. She knew what she was experiencing wasn't real, not exactly. Rather it was a kind of hyper-awareness, her brain taking in each minute detail of a scene and then twisting it, interpreting it in some predaceous relation to herself. And yet still even recognizing it did not lessen this perception; on the contrary it only became more acute as time passed, until every form became a caricature of itself, and every movement a threat she experienced as an actual physical blow. She stopped attending her classes, left her room only to visit the bathroom or the corner store, furtively and after dark, subsisting on granola and fruit and yogurt, which stayed good for a week on her windowsill. She began having flashbacks again, hideous and half-imagined scenes of her assault that her mind birthed and then refused to recall, blanking them out as soon as they arrived. She stopped drawing rather than foster the paranoias that took shape on every page, only to find the four blank walls of her room becoming the canvas for her disintegrating mental state.

It was in this condition that she pulled a tab from an ad outside the corner store for a furnished studio apartment in Queen's Village. Over winter break she moved in, paying for it with a refund of the remaining portion of the year's tuition that her parents had already paid. Everything in it was dirty and broken and cockroaches swarmed the sink at night, but there at least she could lie on her bed and hear the cars drive by outside her window and feel completely anonymous. She didn't enroll in any classes for the spring semester. Instead she prowled the city streets with her head down and music pounding in her ears, always the same Los Van Van album, until she'd internalized every second of its pulsing sound and like an anesthetic it kept her from feeling anything else. At night she dreamed she was still walking, but no matter how far she went it was never far enough. "We feel your pain," a guy shouted at her once from the other side of the street in North Philly, and she almost crossed to him, hoping he could explain it to her. But she never stopped, not for anything, not until the day she took a shortcut through a junkie park and found a box of kittens in the weeds.

Because she no longer trusted her own observations, it took

a few minutes of peering to convince herself they were real. This was late March and the temperature still fell to freezing some nights; it looked like they'd tried to pile together for warmth. The bodies on top were stiff and glass-eyed, but there was movement at the bottom and when she dug down underneath them there were two little bellies, rising and falling.

Two puffs of black and caramel with white tufts between their paws and fluffy ruffs around their neck and kohl-rimmed eyes. She fed them with an eyedropper ten times a day. Then when they were bigger she fed them kibble from her fingers, and every sting of their needle teeth was a reason for continuing to exist. She played and ate and slept with them all that spring and summer, imagining she was half-cat herself. She regarded with some trepidation the boy cat developing a friendly and inquisitive nature, and became extremely protective of the girl cat, who shot beneath the bed at any loud noise, even random voices on the street. The only human she trusted was Laurelie, but she trusted her completely, lying boneless while Laurelie stroked her belly and throat and the fine birdlike bones of her legs, all those vulnerable places on a body that even the gregarious boy cat kept out of Laurelie's reach.

Spending all their lives in one small room was not good for any of them, she knew, and so even as her kittens grew into cats she began the process of transferring to another school, her only criteria that it be far away, and not cost more than the year of tuition money she had left.

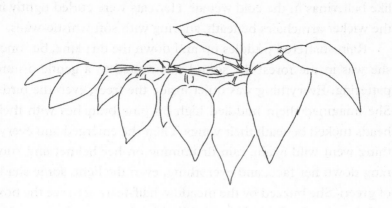

4

Laurelie dreamed she found a box in the meadow on the river road, inside it a mewling mass of fur bathed in light. She wanted to save them but try as she might couldn't figure out a way to attach the box to her bike. She was plucking long grass in order to braid it when a shadow blotted out the sun. But looking up she encountered only blackness where the face should have been. Then panic swamped her and she was on her bike riding away and waking up to wind gusting rain onto her skin.

Her bedroom windows were propped wide open with the weathered sticks of wood she'd found tucked in the sashes when she first moved in. Gauzy white curtains billowed from them like ballerinas in the cold wet air. Her cats were curled tightly in the wicker armchairs beneath, snoring with soft whistle-wails.

Rain shattered puddles up and down the dirt lane, but once she was in the forest the sound was muted to a gentle distant pattering. Everything was quiet inside the trees, even the birds. She imagined them huddled high on pine branches with their heads tucked beneath their wings. Then she emerged and everything went wild again, rain drumming on her helmet and running down her face, and everything, even the light, some shade of green. She buzzed by the meadow, half-fearing to see the box, and then hit the final hill hard. Climbing it, she paid no mind to the fraternity houses, too busy going over her *Bobcat* panels again in her mind. She'd based them on Gauguin's Tahitian paintings, using his broad strokes of vivid color and heavily outlined shapes to capture the stark savagery of the bobcat's swollen belly and bloodied flank. The hiker had come out cat-like as well, following the beast across the panels, both of them moving with silent expertise through a forest where ice still lingered in spring's shadow. The panels, she thought, were nearly finished, but for the thought bubbles above the heads. Right now they were empty, because she hadn't figured out what to put inside them yet. She'd looked up bobcats online. According to the blogs they were territorial and predatory, and capable of taking down prey up to eight times their size. Interactions with them almost invariably led to bites and scratches, often with nasty consequences of infection and disease. So what was the hiker thinking to be following a pregnant and injured one? And why, for that matter, did it not perceive him as a threat?

"You're an art major, right?"

Laurelie halted at the classroom door, unsure if the person was talking to her. Even without turning she recognized the linguistics major's voice. It would have been impossible not to. Since the term started he'd spent half of each language philosophy class debating fine shades of meaning with the professor while the rest of the class quietly shifted and groaned. Laurelie, who was only taking the course to fulfill a senior elective requirement, didn't mind these discussions; their sparring was sometimes interesting, and as long as they talked no one paid any attention to her.

So why was he talking to her now?

"I've been thinking about Wittgenstein's argument that all descriptions are finite and therefore idealizations," he said, coming around beside her. "I think it means he sees art as a language too. If so, then his private language argument would apply to art as well. And I'm wondering if you agree that this would actually be saying something pretty significant, namely that if no one understands a piece of art, then it's not really art at all."

She listened with her head down and her hair hanging around her face, hoping that would make him go away. When he didn't she shrugged, and then when still he stayed she finally mumbled, "Even a single line on a page can mean a lot of things. A single letter on a canvas can be art." Feeling her cheeks growing heavy as bricks, she left the room and, crossing the entry hall at a near run, headed for the outer door.

But the linguistics major kept pace. "Wow, so once you start combining things, the possibilities must get really complex. But still, there are rules, aren't there? There must be some way to distinguish good and bad art."

Hand on the door handle, an expression she'd heard once

flashed into her mind. "Learn the rules and then break them carefully. That's how people make good art." She said it and then pushed, and the sun flooded in. It had sliced through the dark rain clouds and was bursting through, and the sliver of sky behind them was a perfect blue. And into this scene the linguistics major's startled laugh rang out, lending to it for an instant an air of miracle.

He kept up with her as she crossed the green toward her bike, oblivious to her desire to be alone, too intent on following the line of his argument. If Wittgenstein was right, he mused, then nothing about art could really be private. Because if art was a visual language then that meant everyone saw the same things, unless of course they were insane or hallucinating, and even that would only be a distortion. And she found that she understood him, and that this understanding, combined with the sound of his voice and the feeling of the sun shining down, formed a kind of weaving that both insulated her from the threat he posed but also held her captive there beside him. And so she opened her mouth and said right but art was something you had to learn before you understood it. Take Warhol's Monroes, she said, for example, which weren't really about the woman at all, but rather about how images were perceived, how there was no unmediated access to anything, not even your own face.

Then they turned onto the alley and there was the little pub and her bike and the general store. And he said, "Hey, do you want to get something to eat? Or even just a drink."

A heavy bank of clouds now blotted out the sun. The air turned cold, the alley dark and twisted. She looked at her bike, parked in front of her general store, and longed to run to it, to hop on and pedal away.

She looked back at the linguistics major. At the maleness her eye detected emanating everywhere from him. Then, for a moment, she saw beneath it not predation at all but a harmless cub-like nascence. She saw a furry head and myopic eyes that never totally focused, stooped shoulders and a soft belly and a pale fuzz over unmuscular limbs.

A drop of rain hit her cheek, another splatted on the ground. She took one step. And then another.

When she entered the pub, the smell of beer assailed her. The far wall receded, and the voices swelled to a roar as she followed the linguistics major to a table. Sinking down onto a chair she stared at the scarred and polished tabletop, feeling the room pulse and whirl, focusing on controlling her breaths so that her heart wouldn't pound itself right out of her chest. He was talking but she couldn't understand the words and when she looked up his Adam's apple rising and falling appeared as something so mechanical that she had to look down again. The waitress came and he ordered, but it was all that she could do to shake her head. Then he rose and said something and left the table and her eyes followed as if tied to him by string until he disappeared through a door beyond the bar. Bathroom, she realized, and the simply rationality of this thought calmed her enough that she began shallowly processing the peripheral space. A nearby table of older women talking and laughing, two blonds and two brunettes, administrative types in pastel suits and low chunky heels. Another one full of students, freshmen by their look. And up at the bar, a handful of men, who might all have been the same man, hunched over their pint glasses in faded T-shirts with letters peeling off their backs, their working-man pants stained and creased and battered boots on their feet.

Then with a series of depth-charged shocks her brain isolated a black mass of curls. Broad shoulders. Impossibly long folded limbs. And upon this body that had isolated itself from all the rest, she settled her gaze. Her mind channeled all the supple grace that lay stored in its coils like potential energy, fed upon it in order to return to itself, secure in the knowledge of being itself unperceived. But when her eyes grazed the mirror behind the bar, she discovered his eyes were fixed upon her as intently as hers were on him. And for a minute it seemed as if they even breathed as one, for his nostrils reflected back exactly the rise and fall of her own breast.

The linguistic major sat down then, blocking her view, and she was looking down at the tabletop again. But she was still herself, though with a torn apart feeling now, that of once again breathing alone.

"If art is a language it would explain why we can recognize someone's work even when seeing a piece for the first time," the linguistics major said, and she realized she could understand him again.

After the waitress arrived with his meal and a glass of water for her, she looked up. Leaning out a little she saw the bar stool where the hiker had been sitting was empty, and realized something else.

The bobcat had stopped running.

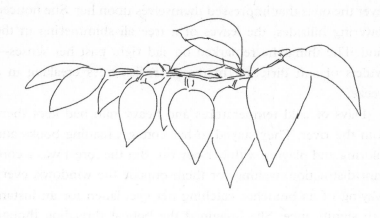

5

The boy had begun seeking order in things. To this end he'd invented a new game. He'd point to an object and she would name and describe it. A blade of grass was green and bendy, a beetle hard and black and quick. He absorbed these new concepts effortlessly, but was still frustrated by his attempts to communicate. The problem, she thought, was that his mouth could yet only shape a few sounds, and each therefore had to be overloaded with meanings. Like how "daa" could be a sound of affirmation, but it could also mean "dog," or that he wanted to be put down, and he used it when he was pointing to something as well. She found it helped to bend down low and try to see from his point of view. Still the things that interested him were never the ones that impressed themselves upon her. She noticed flowering hillsides, the leaves of a tree all shimmering in the wind. The things he remarked on slid right past her senses— rivulets of soft dirt, wet marks on rocks, trees creaking in a breeze.

Days of cold temperatures and heavy rain had kept them from the river. They stayed in her cottage, reading books and coloring and playing with her boy cat. But the forest was a constant distraction, waiting for them outside the windows, every swaying of its branches catching her eye, laden for an instant with significance. She imagined the bobcat threading though the pines just out of sight, watching their movements too through the glass. She wondered if it—*if she*—had given birth yet, whether she still came down to the river to drink, and how often. While the boy colored in outlines of cats, she drew the hiker in the bar with Guston's cartoonish simplicity, his nose over-large and pulsing rhythmically. But still the thought bubbles above his head did not reflect what went on in his mind, only the bar mirror behind him, and in that was an image of her own panicked face.

Then one day the sky was overcast but the air was warmer and the rain did not fall. Her morning classes were strangely empty and the afternoon ones were apparently canceled, for even the professors didn't show up. Looking down Main Street the shops and cafes were deserted, and so was the intersection with High where she waited for her light. She felt disoriented by this and a little afraid, like there was something important happening and she was the only one not aware of it. Then suddenly she smelled perfume, the human kind, a scent of floral shampoos and musky colognes that mingled sourly with the lilac-drenched breeze. Turning her head she saw a crowd of students surging toward her across the green. The girls were teetering in high heels and wearing dresses that exposed great swaths of turgid flesh, while the guys strode awkwardly in shiny shoes, thrusting their hips as if venereal threats lay hidden beneath their suits. And now the pieces all fell into place, and she understood. It was spring formal night at the fraternity houses.

The sky glowered, beetle-browed, as she hurried down the trail, short of breath but with an idea flowering now inside her black mood. The boy in her arms held on tightly but, as if he felt the turbulence inside her, made no sound.

When they reached the river it was the same color as the sky.

"Daa," the boy said, pointing toward Thinking Rock, but she didn't stop, just hoisted him higher on her hip and made for the stretch of ferns from which they'd first seen the bobcat come. She found as she crossed it that it was larger than it had appeared, and the plants that comprised it were so high and dense they hid everything below her knees. The boy twisted in her arms, taking everything in, but made no attempt to get down.

Eventually the ferns thinned, driven through by rocks and branches, and now the trees crowded in, making a canopy that blocked out the sky. With no trail to follow, she simply continued on, and before long a clearing appeared. Oval-shaped, its floor was thick with bright orange pine needles, its borders enforced by tall trunks in single files, their lower limbs black stumps while the uppermost ones still whirled alive, green and feathery, high above her head.

The river had followed them, wrapping itself around the

land, hugging tightly to the edge of the clearing closest to them, which sloped down steeply to meet it. At the far end of the clearing, near where the trees took up again, was a tent. It looked anachronistic there, like something out of the Civil War era, made as it was of bare canvas, with a long triangular prism shape. From its closest face a low awning protruded, held up by two of the fallen pine branches. It looked long ago deserted, and the clearing around it so quiet and still only emphasized the feeling that they'd not only traveled deeper into the woods than they'd ever been before, but also that they'd traveled back in time.

"Daa." The boy wriggled in her arms, and slowly she lowered him to the ground. But barely had he touched it when there came an explosive flurry of sound and she snatched him up again. A dog hurtled past them, bounding down the slope to the river, and shortly thereafter reappeared at the top with a ball in its mouth. It shook itself, sending water droplets flying from its black fur before trotting over and dropping the ball at her feet.

"Daa!"

"Yes, that is a dog. It seems friendly, I guess. Do you want me to throw its ball?"

The boy nodded.

Still holding him, she bent and picked up the dog's toy. It watched her, panting cheerfully. The ball was sodden and appeared homemade, fashioned out of what she thought was the same canvas as the tent. Neatly bisected by fat string stitches, it was packed inside with what felt to her fingers like beans. She tossed it lightly into the clearing, and the dog scrambled after it.

The boy wriggled. "Daa!"

"Okay," she said, letting him down again. "But don't touch it."

Despite her admonition, the moment the dog came trotting

back the boy grabbed two handfuls of the hair along its back. Laurelie hurried between them but the dog only sat, and suffered the subsequent slaps and pats with a panting smile. The boy even captured its thick tongue once and it only slipped the pink flesh back into its mouth before immediately loosing it again, much to the boy's delight. After inspecting its black-speckled gums and teeth, the boy wanted to throw it the ball himself. Although most of his efforts landed behind him, still the dog went after them, circling them with close quick strides that made the boy reach for her legs and squeal.

Rain abruptly ended their play.

"Time to go," she said with a glance at the sky, but even as she spoke, it began to come down hard.

The boy grimaced, trying to wipe the rain from his face and eyes.

"It's only water," she said, bending to take him in her arms, "but we're going to have to run now, okay?"

"You can wait in here. It won't last long."

She nearly ran then, seeing the hiker crouched beneath the awning of the tent. But the escalating whimpers of the boy in her arms punctured the swell of her own fear, so that instead of the trees, she ran for the awning.

She scrambled beneath it, but it was too small to shelter them all. With rain drumming on her back, she hesitated only a moment, then pushed the boy through the curtain of doors and followed him inside. Her first impression was of warmth and spaciousness. As wide as the height of a man, the tent was twice that long, and high enough at its center for her to stand, with deep shadowy corners where the ceiling came low. Apart from some bundles and things at the back, it appeared mostly empty.

She hardly had time to take this in, however, for now the

hiker's large dark body filled the opening. He seemed to take up so much space that she gathered the boy and backed as far into the corner as she could go. But the hiker came no farther; rather he turned around and crouched at the door with his back to them and began tying the door flaps open.

Soon the whole front of the tent gaped wide. Cold wet air blew in, but she welcomed it. The canvas walls and floor were surprisingly dry, and this close she could see why; they had been painted with wax. She could actually follow the stripes of the brush, and for a moment imagined she smelled honey.

Eyes wide, the boy pressed his hand to the wall behind her. It was vibrating visibly beneath the hard rain. Now she became aware of the drumming sound, so loud it swamped her at first with its physical pulse. But slowly other sounds wove through. Her own heart, and then the boy's breaths, and finally a shallow panting sound she believed was the dog until she located it beyond the hiker, curled beneath the awning with its head on its paws, and its mouth closed.

The boy heard it too. He stood in her arms and tried to go, even as she tried to keep him. For a moment they struggled silently before he pulled free and went looking for the dog.

Hardly had he taken a step when the hiker slid through the doorway and folded himself into the shadows of the corner on the other side. Now the empty opening lay before them like a prize, rich with the scents of rain-drenched ground. She followed the boy to it, where he sat in her lap with his hands reaching out through the door, lifting the dog's paws and touching their black tufts of fur, their dry malleable pads and dull curves of nail, while she softly spoke their names and salient features, feeling in the familiar game a palliative, even as the hiker's presence magnified every detail.

Then somehow the boy had slipped from her grasp and was entirely out the door, scuttling toward the end of the awning and the branches that held it up. But even as she realized this, the hiker was sounding a low whistle, and the dog rose and blocked the boy. Gently it herded him back to her, the boy giggling every time their bodies brushed, and once he was safely back in her arms the dog lay down on the ground in front of him with a contented sigh.

"Thanks," she said, after a while.

"Sure."

His voice was low, clipped. Close. Now the confines of the tent drew nearer. As a kind of calming exercise she forced herself to recall exactly what was behind her. The floor, she remembered, was mostly bare, nothing scattered or piled, just a sleeping bag and a hiking pack against the far wall. In her mind's eye these were made of the same canvas as tent and ball, even down to the same neat fat stitching. Except the top of the sleeping bag had been folded over—and now her mind began to whirl, resolving the turned-down layer to a dark, shining fur. She tried to stifle a shiver, felt her clothes suddenly clammy on her skin. Imagined him silently approaching. Waited until she could take it no more, and then in one swift motion, turned and looked at him.

Returning her gaze out the door, his after-image burned against the backdrop of rain. He sat cross-legged in the shadowed corner with his hands in his lap, and they had fisted as her gaze passed over him. His bones in the storm light were as sharp as knife edges, and his eyes had been watering and his nostrils had been flared as white as two sails in a strong wind. His lips had been parted and now she could hear it; he was mouth-breathing again.

The air felt wonder-struck after the rain. She limped with the boy over the bright saturated needles, her legs cramped after sitting in the same position for so long. From behind them came a loud zipping sound, and she glanced back to see one slanted wall of the tent slide halfway down. *Airing us out,* she thought, for the effect was that of an enormous window, and still giddy with the sense of reclaimed freedom, she had to fight back an urge to laugh crazily.

Halfway to the edge of the clearing a whooshing sound above their heads had them both looking up, just in time to see the ball soaring down the slope of the riverbank. In the next instant the dog was racing after it, and the boy was catapulting himself between her knees. When the dog reappeared, dripping, grinning, the boy ran to it. It trotted back to the hiker, who then threw the ball once more, sending both boy and dog back her way again.

She stood watching them racing this way and that, taking in the dog's muddy paws, the boy's muddy clothes, the streaks of mud on the hiker's own pants, the simple cloth and cut of which suggested they too were homemade. She took in the clearing and the river around it, this space he had made his temporary home. She wondered where the bobcat was hidden, if it was watching them right now. She imagined that when she and the boy left it would come out for dinner. She imagined the hiker sitting before a campfire, with his dog on one side of him and his bobcat on the other. She imagined three skinned rabbits roasting on spits, and then hurriedly blocked this image with another, one of them in the morning, walking together down to the river to bathe. Then she spoke all in a rush, seeking a nonchalance her voice belied. "So did the bobcat have its kittens yet?"

"She did." The hiker's reply was almost too low to hear.

"Oh. Well, if you have laundry you need to do . . . or anything . . ."

Flushing hard, she lowered her head so that her hair covered her face, and went after the boy.

They'd reached the trees before the hiker answered.

"Sure," he said. "Okay."

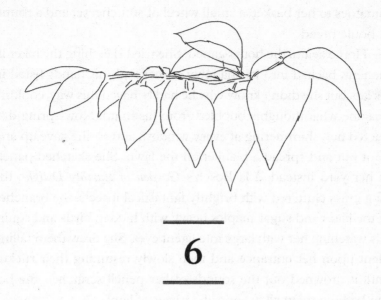

6

Sunday dawned without a fleck of cloud. The sky was blue and the land was fluorescing green after so much rain. All the trees were blooming or dropping seeds, their bright lace covering the river road, scattering into swirls and eddies as Laurelie swept past on her bicycle. Inside the little general store she wandered the aisles. She was no chef, and even an image of a home-cooked meal escaped her now. The slabs of raw meat edged in thick fat rebuffed her, as did the whole fish with their shiny dead eyes. But the shrimp looked somewhat interesting, and easy enough besides, already peeled and steamed after being freshly caught that morning from, of all places, Maine. Now thinking in terms of circles, she was able to flesh out the rest, adding plump tomatoes to her basket, a small wheel of soft cheese, and a round of boule bread.

Home again, the hours gaped. She tried sketching the hiker in the tent, backed into its shadowy corner with his hands fisted in his lap, but she didn't know why he had behaved this way, couldn't imagine what thoughts bubbled from his mind. Now spring distracted her, shimmering at every window, and so she gave up and went out and spread a blanket on the lawn. She sketched panels of her yard instead, à la Bosch's *Garden of Earthly Delight,* the long grass cluttered with brightly fantastical insects, the branches of the lilacs and sugar maples heavy with hidden birds and squirrels watching her with large intelligent eyes. She drew them falling silent upon her entrance and then slowly resuming their ruckus until it drowned out the sounds of her pencil scratches, the hot sun bathing them all in soporific waves of light.

The boy cat woke her later, meowing from the window behind her head. He lay pressed against the screen with his fur poking through it like soft quills, and he licked her finger, making a rasping sound when she touched it to the place where he pressed his nose.

The sun had passed behind the pines and the air had cooled. Her body felt like it had melted and hardened again, her brain like she was still dreaming, and she trembled with a ramping anticipation neither vessel could contain.

She took a hot shower and emerged fluid again, fully stoked in fact, glowing and glistening as she put on fresh jeans and a T-shirt and then ran down the stairs on lightning feet. She'd left the front door open and the evening air stealing in through the screen had drawn her cats from their window perches to investigate. She was sitting on the bottom stair stroking their bellies when the porch stairs creaked.

Like a shot, the girl cat disappeared up the stairs.

When the hiker appeared at the screen door, Laurelie very nearly followed her. The air around him seemed to sparkle and crack, and even after looking down she still felt as if she were being struck by electrical shocks, over and over again.

"Stay, Asa," he said softly. Laurelie heard the dog's soft sigh as it settled down on the porch floorboards.

"Laundry's this way," she said, standing quickly as he opened the door.

He looked down at his boots. "I was wondering," he said, almost too quietly to hear, "if I could shower first. It's been a while since I've felt hot water."

She nodded jerkily. "Okay. But that's upstairs."

Once he stepped inside, her body would not remain still. Despite intense effort she continued to shake as, with slow careful movements, he propped his pack beside the door and then removed his hiking boots. He kept his head down with his dark hair falling over his face, and gave her a wide berth as he moved past her and climbed the stairs, but still not until the bathroom door had closed behind him did she breathe, and then she did so with great wheeling gasps, dizzy from both the lack of air and the receding sense of danger.

His pack and boots freshened the threat each time her roving eyes fell there, but she forced herself to keep looking back at them and so was slightly desensitized to it by the time he returned. She found moreover it helped to keep some part of her always moving, not only the eyes but an extremity too, a shoulder circling, a finger drumming a beat on her thigh, and so in this way as he came toward her down the stairs she absorbed in small doses the hair the water had tamed dripping in coils down his neck, the fresh clothes he wore, and the old ones in his hand.

It was his feet that broke her again, bare now and long and a paler, cooler shade than the rest of him, incredibly intimate, flexing there on the stairs. She turned and made for the kitchen in a body no longer her own. The boy cat, who'd been eating kibble in there, leapt onto the bench of the worn wooden table and meowed. But hearing the hiker coming behind her she did not stop to pet him. She kept going until she hit the cracked formica counter and then, wrapping her arms tightly around her staccato heart, she turned around.

The hiker stopped in the doorway. After setting his pack on the floor, he rubbed a slow index finger over the boy cat's ear. The cat raised its chin for him, and scraped first one cheek and then the other against his palm. Laurelie looked down then, feeling inside her the kicks of small demented creatures, and squeezed herself even more tightly to hold them in.

There came a rustle of canvas, a clink and a snap, and she raised her gaze in time to see the hiker remove the cap from a second green glass bottle with the pad of his thumb.

Keeping his own eyes lowered, he leaned slowly forward and placed it on the end of the table near her, then stepped back again. Picking up the other bottle, he drank long and deep, not stopping until it was almost gone.

The kicks grew frantic as she stared at her bottle. Unseeing at first, slowly her eyes focused, and she read the label: Mead. Written on a plain white label in a tightly curling script, it made the bottle appear archaic, like something unearthed from a long-buried trunk. Even the word sounded ancient as it reverberated in her head, mystical, almost an incantation. *Maybe it is*, she thought, and then took the bottle in shaking hands and drank.

The first sip was biting and sweet. It slid down her insides and dulled the kicks there. The next one pooled, a liquid center of calm that spread to her limbs as she sipped again.

"This way," she said, moving down the small hallway toward the laundry room. Entering, she heard him behind her, mouth-breathing in shallow pants and, suddenly realizing she'd been trapped, she backed in deep and pressed her back to the wall, raising her bottle before her like a wand or a weapon. But when his large body filled the doorway he didn't even look at her. Setting a fresh bottle of mead on the dryer and his pack on the ground, he began loading clothes from it into her washing machine. She took another sip of the mead. When he was done he set the dials and closed the lid with two fingers so that it made no sound, then picked up his own bottle and drained it.

The washer started up with a *rumble-whoosh*, startling them both.

"There's soap," she said.

He shook his head. "Hot water works fine."

She told him she'd bought food but didn't really like to cook. He said he did. And then he opened a third bottle of mead and stood at her fridge with his nostrils going light-speed. After a while he began pulling things out, the shrimp, her yogurt, a few carrots, an apple. He started opening her drawers and cupboards next, rustling through them for a pot, a cutting board, a large knife he thumbed and frowned over before putting it back again. After adding a few inches of water to the pot, he set it to heat on the stove. Once it was boiling he lifted the tomatoes by their vine and, grimacing as if they burned, dropped them inside. Tears leaked from his eyes and he wiped them on his sleeve with a practiced motion before fishing them out again. He did the same with the carrots and the apple, and then rinsed the pot thoroughly and set it to heat again. His face had settled into a kind of pulse as he worked, but there was an anticipation to it as well, she thought, an expectation that she would eventually speak and disturb his rhythm. But the shapes of her own observations were too delicate to upset. *Heat,* she thought, *sterilize,* watching the steam rise from the produce on the cutting board. She didn't flinch when he slipped from his front pocket a long wooden-handled buck knife and proceeded to rough-chop and julienne the blanched produce, too focused on the thin ribbons curling up, the silvery blur of his blade. And when she lifted her bottle to her lips and found that it was empty, already he was opening two more.

Then, reaching deeper into his pocket, he pulled out a small brown paper bag and poured from it a handful of paper twists, which he laid out on the table. He selected certain ones seemingly at random and twisted them open to reveal their insides. Bright red threads, golden crystals, a long shriveled black bean. *Potion,* she thought as he sprinkled these into his pot, his nostrils rippling now with irregular vibrations.

Something brushed her ankle as he stirred, and crooning in surprise, she bent down and scooped up the girl cat, who settled into her favorite spot, draped over Laurelie's shoulder like a scarf, purring like a gravelly pump.

The kitchen was warm and smelled of the sea, but the porch was cool and smelled of night flowers. The dog's tail thumped once when she set down the bowl of water, but other than that she wouldn't have known it was there, for its black fur had rendered it invisible. Across the lane the forest was depthless, just a blacker silhouette against the night. A yellow quarter moon hung above it, full of shadows. She imagined its weak glow was a capsule, inside which she could move without impediment, and the stoked heat she'd felt before the hiker arrived stirred once more, deep inside her, but molten now, and slow. There was no single instant when she became aware of him behind her; it was more of a slow fusion, and then suddenly her heart was racing to handle the extra weight.

"It's ready," he said then, and pushed open the screen door.

There were two bowls in his hands, one of which he held out to her. His nostrils were flared hard, and she thought, *Smelling me,* and then felt the heat inside her bloom and spread its slow tendrils all the way up to her head and down to her feet.

They ate on the porch but it felt like a restaurant, for never had she tasted anything so good. *Creamy leather bellies, sweet mermaid legs*—her mind flashed images attempting to match the flavors in her mouth as she mopped up the last rich pools of sauce with bread.

After that it became necessary to recline. Even before her mind had fully processed the determination she was lying on the couch. Her head felt so heavy she imagined it as a planet revolving on her neck, so that first she had to close one eye, and then the other, in order to see straight. She kept the open one always on the hiker, who was revolving some distance away, lying down on the floor beside the open front door with his head resting on his pack and his long legs splayed.

It was some time before she put together the focus of his gaze and the rhythm of his nose with the noises coming from her ancient TV. "What're we watching?" she said then, and when, after a startled instant, he laughed—*wide mouth dark, a perfect audience of teeth*—she felt the throb of victory like violence.

Whatever name he gave, she watched it. But in the morning when she woke still on the couch he was gone, and all she could recall were vivid snapshots, a cheerless prison, a man eating too many hard-boiled eggs, then fighting a giant, then digging the same hole over and over again, and then finally dying.

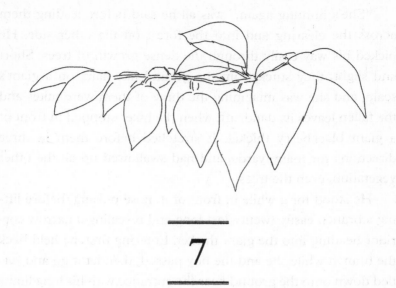

7

The boy insisted on walking this time. Some of the ferns rose higher than his head, tickling him so that he giggled the whole way through. Being with him made her almost remember what being a child was like, when every sensation felt new. She wondered if this was anything like what the hiker experienced too. A week had passed before she dared go back but still it was as if he knew, for he and the dog were waiting for them at the edge of the pine clearing. When the boy ran to meet them, he stuck his hands deep in his pockets and lifted his shoulders but he smiled, a one-corner smile that made her flush, and though his eyes never rose to see it she imagined he knew, from the way his nostrils pulsed.

"She's hunting again," was all he said before leading them across the clearing and into the forest on the other side. He picked his way easily through the dense growth of trees. Short and slight, they stuck from the ground like hairs on a giant's scalp, and she was imagining the three of them were mites and the fallen leaves its dandruff, when the hiker stopped in front of a giant blackberry thicket. It stretched before them in three directions for many yards, and had swallowed up all the other vegetation, even the trees.

He stood for a while in front of it, nose pulsing, before lifting a branch easily twenty feet long and revealing a narrow corridor heading into the giant thicket. Entering first, he held back the branch while she and the boy passed, then let it go and settled down onto the ground near the entrance with his long limbs folded in. After a little hesitation she sat too, with the boy in her lap staring all around at the woody vines sprouting tiny white flowers and sharp thorns.

The hiker had his head turned away from them and was watching a large mossy boulder some yards further along the passage, behind which the thick twining heart of the thicket grew. Suddenly half a dozen striped bundles came tumbling over it, their tiny tails whirling like propellers and the black stripes on their faces smiling like Charlie Chaplin masks. She stared, heart in her throat, as they scaled the hiker's limbs, some clawing their way up his pants to his lap, others climbing his shirt to his shoulders. One ventured out to the end of his knee and stretched out its nose, black and trembling, to the boy, who laughed breathlessly as his face was explored. That bob-kitten soon dashed away but more followed now that the first had dared, darting up and down them too in a cascade of quivering, shivering fur. The boy's face was lit with wonderment, but the hiker's moved like an orchestra as he gazed down at the bob-kitten in his lap and stroked its ears with a long brown thumb.

At first she mistook their mother for a bird. Not until the high-pitched chirrups that called the bob-kittens home had ended and they were back behind the rock did it occur to Laurelie that the bobcat must have been there the whole time, just a few feet away from her, and by then it was too late to feel afraid.

She let the gap widen as she followed the hiker back through the trees. *When*, she thought as the boy ranged between them, racing first to catch up with the hiker and then running back to her. *When*, she thought once the clearing was winking through the trees.

The hiker crouched and the boy ran to him. Together they examined something on the forest floor. After the hiker stood and went on again the boy carried it proudly back to her. It was a feather, but no ordinary one; this one was as long as her forearm, and striped horizontally with black and white alternating bands. "Tur," the boy told her confidently, "tur, tur." Then he ran after the hiker with it still clutched tightly in his fist. *When*, she wondered, watching the hiker come to the boy with his canvas ball and show him how to throw it underhand, so that it rose high and the dog leapt for it, jaws snapping, black body twisting, catching it just before it hit the ground. *When*, she thought, once the sun dropped behind the pines and it was time to take the boy home again. *When will he go?*

That evening she stood at her screen door looking out at the pines awash in pink light, and saw him coming up the trail, the dog at his heels. Quickly she stepped back against the wall. She held very still and made no sound but when he reached the screen door she heard him mouth-breathing and knew that he knew. Between the sounds of his breaths she could hear leaves shimmering, and it seemed as if his breath stirred them too.

There was a store-bought roasted chicken breast in her fridge, which he proceeded to chop into parts and sauté on her stove along with some dried yellow peels from his paper twists and a sprig of a plant growing against the side of her house that she'd always assumed was a weed. But his nose spasmed arrhythmically as he cooked and he made his way steadily through three bottles of mead. And when the meal was ready he didn't touch it. Rather, he stood at the counter drinking more mead while she sat at the table eating without tasting, until the silence grew as terrible as a bad chord ringing and she wished that he would leave.

Then he did, or tried to, but he stumbled on the porch stairs and fell down into the dirt, with the dog nosing around him anxiously. Seeing it, she ran to help, and he reared up with both hands as if it were she that would hurt him, and his face worked so painfully she no longer wanted him to go.

"Stay," she whispered, "please stay," and once he was slumped on her floor in the breeze from the door with his nose pulsing hectically she turned on her TV. She got the dog some water and some of the chicken and then found another old movie, a Hitchcock this time, about a man who watched others though the window. She didn't like it much, but the hiker seemed riveted, the slow beat of his nose hypnotic, narcotic, his eyes hanging from the screen like plum weights. As soon as the credits rolled the lids drifted closed, but beneath them his eyes still moved, and so did his nose.

On silent feet then, she ran up the stairs. She found her sketchbook and, returning to the hiker, sitting closer to him than she'd ever been before, began rapidly filling in panels. The same form again and again, drawn with a Rembrandt-like psychological intensity, the same long bones and same capping joints, the same clavicle sharp and instrument-like with its two straight bones and two round ones, her mind playing harmony to the dip in between that throbbed faintly with his every heartbeat. In each panel his sleeping form remained the same; only his face changed, responding to minute air currents and barely audible sounds and infinitesimal changes of light, along with countless other stimuli her senses never even perceived and of which she was only made cognizant by observing his. These, finally, were what filled his thought bubbles—not even thoughts at all but simply all the great quantity of physical stimuli he was receiving, magnified and analyzed, broken down by his body into chemicals and geometries, molecules and coordinates, billions of tiny, perfect subatomic particles.

In the morning the idea came to her. She was in her language philosophy class, the final one of the term. They'd moved on in their final weeks of the semester to theories of illocutionary acts—how a language, used in certain ways, could perform actions, could actually *do* something—and now such an act in the language of art was whispering to her skin with each shift of the silk she wore beneath her clothes while she sat on a blanket outside her cottage watching the hiker cook in the ancient stone fire pit tilting on her lawn.

She'd taken the boy to find him again, half afraid he'd

already be gone, and asked him to show her how to use it. That evening, as she'd suspected, he seemed more comfortable outside. He was still on his first bottle of mead—and this was crucial, for both needed enough, but not too much, in order for the act to succeed.

And once the meal was ready, he ate. On another hunch, she'd gotten this chicken from a local organic food market she'd ridden past once while riding north on the river road. He wolfed down two pieces. But he savored the mushrooms she'd also found at that market; they ate these slowly, one by one—shiitake, porcini, morel, bai-ling—and each taste unfurled like its body and name, alien, an epiphany on the tongue.

Afterwards he lay back with his hands behind his head and his whole face gone soft, reflecting the slow emergence of night. She felt brave as she headed inside with the dishes, and coming back to the screen door, looking at the shape of him cast by the porch light on the lawn, she quickly she shed her jeans and T-shirt, dropping them to the floor, and tugged down the short silky slip. The night air was chilly and the thin fabric that was now all she wore felt like ice clinging to her breasts and hips, making her tremble. She'd found it in a thrift store far down the alley, after trying things on for the better part of an hour while the saleslady kept the boy entertained with scarves and boas. But in her mind now the snowy silk was not lingerie at all. It was an exorcism. It was proof the body beneath wasn't forever broken. It was a bridge swinging above a giant crevasse. She pulled open the screen door and watched her body move across the porch, carried along by two strong limbs that were part of her even if she could not feel them, each extension bringing her one step closer to the other side.

But long before she reached the hiker, he raised his head. His nostrils flared and he turned his neck. Just one look, that's all it took, and he was gone.

And then, standing there freezing beneath the weak porch light, she looked down at herself and saw bumps and knobs, blue veins and stray hairs, old scars and fresh bruises. A body that could be wounded but remain alive.

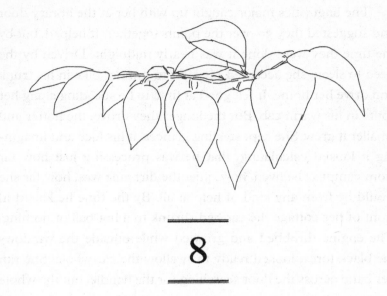

8

She didn't sleep well that night, and in the morning went through the motions, enervated, rising and eating and riding to campus with no sense that what she did was the realest part of her life. It was a perfect crystalline late May day but she hardly noticed, studying in the library for her finals. In the evening she attended a review session for her philosophy exam. Afterward, instead of going home, she headed back to the library, for the professor had spent the entire hour enigmatically pushing peripheral points she hadn't studied well. And while she wouldn't put it past him to purposely muddy the waters, she now had to make sure she understood them because they might appear on her exam tomorrow.

The linguistics major caught up with her at the library door and suggested they go over the points together. It helped, but by the time they were done it was nearly midnight. Driven by the need to sleep, she accepted his offer to put her bike in his trunk and drive her home. It felt good at first, to be speeding along her route in his warm cab. But the longer they drove, the hotter and smaller it grew. She kept stealing glances at his face and imagining it looked calculating, that he was processing just how far from campus she lived, how quiet the dirt lane was, how far she would be from any kind of help at all. By the time he halted in front of her cottage the car had shrunk to a hot ball of nothing. The engine throbbed and growled while outside the windows the black forest looked ready to swallow the car whole. She ran her hand across the door searching for the handle, but the whole expanse felt like one smooth capsule and in her panic she could recognize nothing at all. And then he was on her, his weight suffocating her and his hot breath damp on her neck.

"Here it is," he said, and pushed.

The interior light splashed on, clinical, surgical, as the door swung wide. She spilled out and hurried around to the back of the car. Pulling her bike from the trunk, she dropped it right there on the lawn and sprinted for the porch.

She heard him beep, a friendly bleat, as she pushed through her front door. She stopped then, just over the threshold, as if by magic it made her safe. She listened to the car drive away. And slowly, as the silence became complete, her heart stopped clattering and her breath evened out, and she perceived that she had not been in danger at all. She stood in darkness but it wasn't absolute. Knowledge had density, the arch of the kitchen doorway, the rectangle of couch, the staccato ascent of stairs. Holding out her hands, she walked toward where she knew the light switch would be.

Nearly there, she heard a sound and stopped short. *Mouth-breathing*, she thought and, stomach leaping, felt for the switch and flicked it on, then hurried back out to the porch. But she caught sight of the hiker for only an instant before he slipped beyond the edge of her light.

She dreamed she was in the library stacks, desperate to study all the things she still hadn't learned in the last moments before her exam. But in the aisles all around her other students were talking and laughing as if they already knew all the things she did not, and some were even screaming, and then she was awakening to a cacophony of birds outside her windows.

The clock read 7:54.

At 7:59 she was racing down the dirt lane. Fifteen minutes later she was accepting an exam from her frowning philosophy professor with sweat still trickling down her sides. She felt the stares of the other students as she made her way to an empty seat at the back. But she did not blush. For inside her still pumped the energy of her ride, and she found it could be projected from her like a shield and then, once she sat down, aimed at the page in a single focused beam.

Hours later she rode back up the lane still thinking about the idea of an internal core of energy, and how it could be centered and focused for use both in defense and to forge a connection. She had parked her bike in the yard and was sitting on the porch stairs drawing figures with energies shooting out of their chests and the tops of their heads when the hiker and his dog came up the trail.

Waiting for them, she felt her muscles tensing and her pulse begin to rush, but she kept her eyes hard-focused and controlled her breath, and in this way her brain stayed calm enough to observe, as the hiker got closer, how his own eyes were half-lidded and his nose thickly pulsed and his stride listed a little as he walked. How familiar he seemed, though she'd known him barely a month. How on his back he carried his pack, and it was heavy, with the roll of his sleeping sack tied at the top and his tent tied to the bottom.

A few yards away from her he stopped and shrugged it off, then, looking down at it in the grass, he began to talk. And though the words came out a little slurred, thoughts a little distorted, slowly it emerged that he was describing to her some documentary he'd once seen. Something about a man who went to Alaska and spent the next fifty years living in the wilderness alone. A kind of visual survival manual, he'd filmed the animals he'd found to hunt and fish, the plants he'd found that were safe to eat, and all the stages along the way as he built himself a cabin and everything that went inside it, figuring out what he needed as he went along, like snowshoes and snares and specialized tools and storage units for food and tricks to stop bears from getting into it.

Every so often while he talked, the hiker would take a step closer. One, and then another, with long pauses in between, so she felt a kind of euphoria building in that slow-closing gap, carrying with it all the anticipation of a touch, so that when he finally did touch her there was no shock, only a deep sense of grounding. His hands came up and they were hard and hot, smoothing her shoulders, exerting a gentle pressure through her muscles to the bones beneath. His eyes were closed, and she closed hers too, imagined herself encased in a glacier, great shards of her carving off.

When the dog barked, the hiker's hands dropped away and he stepped back, nostrils flaring.

"Here you are! Rowan's been bouncing off the walls. Finally I had to leave him with the cleaner so I could come down to see what had happened to you."

The landlady was wearing a flowing white dress and a large matching sunhat. In one hand she held a wineglass, the dark liquid pitching as she descended the hill.

"I had exams," Laurelie said, reddening. "I told you I couldn't come today."

"Did you?" The woman stopped and sipped her wine. "Well, I guess they're over." She looked at the hiker appraisingly and, after a moment, smiled. His nostrils flared, but his gaze remained on the ground. "I know," she said, looking back at Laurelie. "Why don't you two come up to the garden for a glass of wine? It's after five. You can keep us company until Rowan's daddy gets home."

For a moment the invitation in her eyes shone brightly. But as Laurelie hesitated, it seemed to morph into something harder, more hostile. And when still Laurelie didn't respond it grew fangs, dripping with hunger and promising pain.

"Sure," said the hiker softly. "I have a little time before my bus."

The thing in the woman's eyes blinked away. She smiled once more at him, but he was still looking down, and there were tears caught now in his downcast lashes.

He left his pack on the porch but kept the dog at his side, which the landlady ignored after a single disdainful glance. She chattered brightly as they climbed the hill but stopped when the landlord's car turned onto the lane. After parking the car, he strode down to meet them. Stocky and sandy-haired, he wore a gray summer suit and burgundy loafers with tassels that made a slapping sound as he walked.

"You're early!" his wife told him tetchily. "They wanted to have a glass of wine with me. Unless you're too tired for company?"

"No, it's fine." He gave a curt nod to Laurelie and then turned to the hiker. "Owen Callis," he said, thrusting out a hand.

The hiker's own hands were thrust deep in his pockets, and there they stayed as he regarded the landlord's hand. His nose began to spasm erratically and his body tensed. If he had a tail it would be puffed and swishing, Laurelie thought, and feared that at any moment he would disappear.

Then the front door of the main house opened, and the boy came barreling down the walk. "Caa caa caa caa caa!" he cried, and Laurelie stepped forward and caught him and lifted him and then turned and pushed him into the hiker's arms. It was the only thing she could think of to do, and she thought after all it was the right thing, for as soon as the boy had settled against him, the hiker's nostrils settled into a strong steady pulse.

The landlord frowned, but the landlady only regarded the hiker again. "Rowan's usually shy of strangers," she said. Then she led the way around the house to the garden in back with her husband following. Laurelie and the hiker came last. The boy's small fingers gripped the hiker's ear as they walked and he leaned close to it, whispering "tur" and "caa."

The landlords left them in the garden and went inside. Soon

the landlady returned with two more glasses of wine. The hiker put the boy down and took one and immediately drank half.

The landlord appeared shortly after with his own wineglass. He had changed out of his suit into a freshly pressed shirt and slacks. "So how are you liking Montague?" he said to the hiker, coming to stand beside his wife.

The hiker raised his glass and finished it.

"He doesn't go to Montague, actually. He's been hiking the AT," Laurelie said quickly.

"Ah!" the landlord said, nodding. "We see a lot of you coming through our little town this time of year."

"I've never understood the thrill of hiking myself," the landlady remarked, wrinkling her nose. "Dirt, bugs, and wild animals. What's there to like about that?"

"Caa," said the boy. He was playing with his trucks in the grass. The dog lay beside him, chin in its paws. The landlady pursed her lips. Laurelie crouched down next to them and wondered how soon they could leave.

Thankfully her landlords seemed to forget all about them after that. They began discussing their new beach house. She told him her countertops still hadn't come in, but at least they'd finally finished the window treatments, and he told her about a fishing boat company he'd found that for a couple hundred took you to a place where you were sure to catch big fish, and they baited the line and chummed the water, so all you had to do was reel 'em in.

As they talked the hiker drifted away to an apple tree and stood watching a formation of swallows dipping and wheeling across the sky. But to Laurelie, it seemed as if he were leading them, as if he were anticipating the birds' changes in course even before they made them, his head predicting their direction a fraction of a second ahead. She remembered the feeling of his touch, and felt relief and loss in equal measure, mingled with joy so fat and buoyant she thought she might actually float away.

Then suddenly the landlord slapped his neck with a startled curse, and the landlady began lighting candles all around the deck. The air filled with a strong scent of citronella. The hiker turned around, and with tears on his cheeks and his nostrils in full flight said quietly, "I have to go now."

"I'll come back for him," he said.

She'd followed him down the hill, and now they stood on her porch, eyeing the dog at his side. She was deliberately not looking at his laden pack, whose pale canvas glowed with such melancholic radiance beneath the moth-struck yellow bulb. She could only nod in response, for her throat had seized at the significance of this material link he was leaving behind. Though in truth there was little alternative, since he'd left his truck three hundred miles north to follow the bobcat more than a month before. And now he was taking a Greyhound bus back to it, on which, despite its name, dogs weren't allowed.

The hiker bent. "Stay, Asa," he murmured, and then touched the dog's head and hefted his pack and walked off down the lane, heading for the river road.

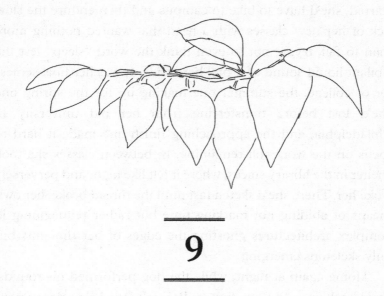

9

In the evening, the hiker's dog marked time. According to some exacting internal interval he would rise and inspect the cottage, high tail slowly sinking as his search came up empty yet again. He ignored her cats, who treated him far less graciously, hissing and swiping at him from the stairs whenever he went by. The reconnaissance continued all night long; from upstairs in her bed Laurelie would wake once more to the click of toenails on floorboards, and half in dream hold her breath as if hoping too, until the dog settled by the front door again with a low drawn-out whine.

Mornings, both were exhausted. The dog would pass out on the front porch, back hairs twitching fretfully, tail thumping feebly whenever Laurelie walked by. The summer semester having just started, she'd have to bike to campus and then endure the slow tick of her new classes with a head that wanted nothing more than to fall, trying not to even think the word "sleep" lest the sibilant liquid sound of it pull her inside. It was her final semester of college, the summer one making up for the spring one she'd lost before transferring from her old university in Philadelphia, and the approaching finish line made it hard to focus on the work still remaining. In between classes she took shelter in the library stacks, where it felt like night and perversely woke her. There she'd sketch fast until the thread broke, her own means of abiding not marking time but rather reimagining it, complex architectures ghosting the edges of her thoughts but only skeletons emerging.

Home again at night, while the dog performed his rounds, she'd back up, add flesh, first to *Bobcat's Den*, half a dozen panels of Escherian recursion in which bob-kittens scaled the hiker's frame and tumbled down again, the thought bubbles drifting above his head graphing their forces and accelerations. And then *Night Flight*, a sequence of Dali-like vistas in which mosquitoes swarmed and candles flared and the hiker was pursued by a cloud of pungent smoke that vaguely resembled her landlady, with his thought bubbles full of symbols for poison and fire and hazardous waste. Though backgrounded in every panel, the hiker's form was triangulated to be its focal point, so that the eye returned to him again and again.

The hours they babysat her landlady's son were the only unalloyed respite from waiting, for both Laurelie and the dog. The boy required all of their combined attention. Fetch was the game now; she'd stroke the stitches of the dog's homemade canvas ball like a talisman beneath her thumb, waiting for the boy to shout "*ray, seh, go!*" and then launch it down the lane as far as she could throw, all three of them experiencing the same fierce rush as the dog released himself, a speeding black projectile. But after every few throws she'd have to outsmart him, changing directions at the last minute, else he would start anticipating her, running even before she threw, and then correspondence would fail them all, the boy shouting *"no baa daw!"* over and over while she waved the ball in the air helplessly, until finally the dog came trotting back.

The dog's presence seemed to be helping the boy; he'd begun speaking much more, even sandwiching together short phrases, which often resonated with mysterious intent. Like *"wok eeen noz,"* which she was relieved to discover referred only to a dry mucus ball; it must have formed up there over a period of days, like a pearl in an oyster. Or *"mow aaaann swee,"* which he intoned for half an hour one afternoon while walking across her porch and striking it rhythmically with a stick. It acted on her and the dog like a soporific, sending them both into a semi-trance, an effect entirely at odds with the ant extermination he was actually performing.

In this way, nine days passed. Then one bright Saturday morning, lying in his usual spot on the porch, the dog saw a truck top a knob in the river road and was off like a shot, reaching the end of the dirt lane just as the vehicle slowed for the turn, and barking and leaping at the driver's side door until it opened and let him in.

Ancient and green, the pickup clattered to a halt in her yard, and wild-hearted she sat on the top porch stair and watched the door open and first the dog pour out and then the hiker. He rubbed his neck and smiled down at the ground, and under the high sun his black curls gleamed blue. In each hand he held a brown paper package. One of these he laid on the truck's hood, and the other he opened to reveal a glistening pink and white marrow bone. The dog rose eagerly to take it, standing on his two hind legs like a trick, so that she thought of the boy in a calming sort of way, and kept thinking of him as the dog ran a dozen mad loops of joy around the man.

But once the dog had settled in the truck's deep shade and was making his first deep noisy cuts, her vision broadened again, deluging her with an accumulation of fresh detail. The motions of the hiker's fingers opening the other package. The angle his neck made bent, as he worked his way in a few starved bites through one half of the enormous sandwich it contained. The depth of umber where his elbow creased as he folded the rest of it carefully away, and the rigid climb of muscle up his sleeve when he stuck his hand through the open truck window and pulled out a new canvas ball. Already the dog was scrambling to its feet and tearing away down the lane, and now she perceived what she hadn't before, that these were the first intricate steps of a ballet. Dog running, hiker waiting, timing it before throwing the ball so low and fast that it shot past the dog and struck the ground exactly a foot ahead, and then the dog snapping it up without ever breaking stride and circling back to drop it at the hiker's feet.

When finally the dog sank panting to his haunches, the hiker bent and stroked his head. Then he walked around to the back of his truck with the dog following so close that leg and flank stayed in constant contact. Reappearing, he held a large potted plant in each hand. He set these down on the bottom porch step.

"I had an African violet once," she said, after a while. A tiny, furred thing, she'd bought it to brighten her dorm room back in Philadelphia. It hadn't done well in that small, dim space. But then again, neither had she.

The hiker's nostrils flared thoughtfully. "They're temperamental. Not these." Lightly he ruffled the head of one plant, releasing a burst of fragrance that seemed too pungent for the yellow florets peeking from its deeply wrinkled leaves. "Water them if they wilt, that's all."

She studied the plants awhile, the way the dark green foliage curled down the stalks, before finally admitting, "They look like they're wilting now to me."

But the hiker only nodded. "It was a long ride."

"Why are you making them so big?"

He was shoveling two holes nearly three feet wide and deep, even though the pots weren't half that size. "Want it loose. Roots shouldn't push. New environment shocks them enough." He breathed around his speech, finishing the holes while she remembered with a physical clarity her own first days in this tiny Vermont town. Ten hours north and the environment had changed so completely. She'd always been cold, and the water had tasted strange, and even breathing had felt wrong, because the air smelled so different.

Kneeling down now, the hiker picked up a plant. Grasping the stalk where it met the soil, he turned it over and gave it a firm tap before twisting it smoothly from the pot. What emerged took her completely by surprise. Countless white roots no larger than hairs had woven themselves as tight as a basket around the dirt, taking on the exact shape of the pot. *Did they grow until they ran out of room, and then stop?* She thought of the hermit crab in the boy's storybook, whose own growth had forced it to leave its shell behind. She wondered what would have happened to it if it had just . . . stayed. *And what would have happened to me?*

"They're the stomach, heart, and brain," the hiker remarked, nose gently flaring as he traced the path of a single tiny root with his thumb. "You can raze a plant all the way to the ground and it won't die. Not unless you get the roots." His voice was soft, proud. She looked at the forest across the lane and imagined all the pine trees as mirror images, half their lives taking place underground. *Hidden,* she thought, *safe.*

The hiker was opening his buck knife now. "Have to cut them or they won't grow," he said, and then made a series of deliberate slices through the sides and bottom of each root ball while she tried not to think of pain.

After loosening the dirt around the cuts, he laid the plants in their holes and scooped back the freshly dug earth, pausing every few handfuls to tamp it down. The soil smelled so good, so rich and round, and she marveled at the sheer quantity of it, at the curled white grubs and long banded worms and black-shelled beetles skittering around. He lined each plant's base with a circle of wood chips, which after the dirt seemed like mere adornment; it wasn't until he'd taken his can to her spigot and was watering the plants that she realized his mulch served a purpose too, forming a barrier so the water collecting in those fragrant basins would soak down into the thirsty earth rather than immediately dispersing.

"So water if they wilt and they won't die on me," she said, as he rose again and brushed his hands on his jeans.

"Not until winter at least." He glanced at her, and then away again, his eyes moistening as if in sympathy. "Tomato plants aren't native to this climate. Their roots don't go deep enough to survive the cold."

Now she was thinking of everything in terms of roots, root systems. Like how she understood that this evening would proceed like all the others had. But also how there was new growth too, pushing up from the cut into the black of possibility. Like riding for groceries in his ancient truck with its ragged leather seats and crank windows and analog dials, Fela calling out injustice through the old dash speakers. And the way the hiker drove so deliberately, with his elbow browning ever deeper out the window and his long spare body fitting perfectly behind the wheel. How he smelled all the produce before putting it in the cart and smiled when she said it would make her feel like a monster now to eat anything at all. How they sat on her porch with pints of strong dark beer and watched the sun descend, lightening surfaces and deepening depths until they appeared almost infinite. She'd thought she couldn't drink beer anymore, but his homemade one went down easy, tasting of dark bread and molasses and mingling with the fragrance-drenched breeze. Long ago someone planted a moon garden here, he told her, and that distant tangle of brush was in fact a thriving colony of night-blooming jasmine and evening stock and primrose, of phlox and gladioli and moonflower. Each time his flickering nose isolated a new perfume he would jog the whole length of the yard to retrieve it, just so she could pair scent and image in her head. And when darkness enveloped them, he planted her at the sink washing produce, which turned out to be the perfect job for her, because she was an integral part of the making of the meal but couldn't ruin it, and moreover could observe all the minutiae of his own process without affecting it either.

It was too buggy to eat outside, as she knew he would have

preferred, so they settled with their meal on her living room floor in the screen door's breeze. Afterward he lay back with his hands behind his head and his eyes closed and his nose gently flaring with each waft of night air. She sat upright beside him, hugging her knees, knowing they'd probably watch an old movie soon. But in that moment even the thought felt too tight, like a too-small shell. A Cuban melody drifted through her head. Once it had played in her ears unceasingly, blocking out the miles of Philadelphia streets she'd walked in the months following her rape. Now, after so long, it called to her again. A root cry, a phoenix song. So she rose and put it on, raised the volume until the very air seemed to ripple and bounce, each beat another cut, another growing pain. Holding her upper body still, she let the rest of herself swing loose, not in a walk now, but a dance. And then she was blushing in a headlong rush because his hands had found her waist and were turning her, barely even touching her and yet the torque of him so strong.

A labyrinth of hallways and stairs. Infinite hallways. Infinite stairs. She'd dreamed of them many times since the frat brother had half-carried, half-dragged her to his room. But now, for the first time, a doorway appeared, out of which spilled the most intense light. She opened her eyes and it was sunlight, pouring on the floor of her living room in her little cottage in Vermont. Pooling on the body next to her.

So close. They lay curved together like a circle halved. Fur-tongued, fluff-headed, she closed her eyes, remembering his hands, his body brushing hers as they danced. Then guzzling water like life force. Lying down on a blanket, looking into each other's eyes, falling asleep to the soft sound of her cats' whistle-wails.

The hiker shifted then, came out of his curl. Opened his eyes.

She mimed sleep but after a while he reached over and took her hand. He brought it to his nose, nudged it open like a flower, and breathed her in.

They sat on the porch, their skins heating in steady increments as the sun inched its head above the pines. The hiker was working his way through the other half of his sandwich while she ate her usual breakfast of yogurt and granola. She was watching the changing velocities of his nose, and wondering what specifically they might reflect, while thinking more generally about how reflections behaved in such a rural place, where there was so much space across which physical stimuli could travel and disperse. So many smells and colors to the earth. So many sounds. So many birds, their calls so complex. So that after a while, because she was thinking all this while looking at him, the silence felt no different than the thoughts in her head, and it hardly seemed she was speaking aloud when she said, "Maybe you were born with it."

He startled then. He shook his head.

Then he rose. He didn't say that she should stay behind, but she could tell by his nose that he felt it. After he and the dog were gone, she imagined the path they took in her head. The trail down to the river and through the fern field and the forest beyond, across the clearing where he'd camped and then into the dense new growth on the other side. But there she stopped short, blocked somehow, as if his bobcat's den were another secret, another shell, another root too deeply bound.

When he returned it was much later. The sun was hitting everything sideways, making it feel hyperreal. She asked after the bobcat; he said her leg was healed. He said the kittens had doubled in size and were starting to catch their own food now. Probably they said other things as well, but the words seemed to travel a great distance, and they arrived without any impact. She felt like she was standing on the surface of Mars as he turned toward his truck and whistled for his dog. Her eyes kept glancing off him as if he wasn't there, and in another minute he really wasn't. There was only the dust stirred up along the lane to prove he'd ever been there at all.

That night she drew *Mars*, and *Moon Garden*, and *Cutting the Roots*. She drew secret paths through labyrinths of forests, riotous flowers, and the sideways rays of alien suns. She drew black dirt spilling through brown fingers, and a million white roots tightly bound. She drew a buck knife, flashing silver in the sun.

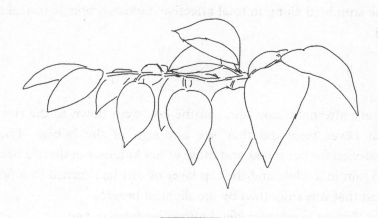

10

As the sun stretched toward its solstice, the bustle of Laurelie's little town grew. Now when she rode to the general store early each morning, the main streets were already full. She imagined the core of energy inside herself was a Tesla coil, sending out shoots, burning holes in her cloak of invisibility, seeking out the other strange circuits that helped power the outside world. And while these egresses felt little worse than pinpricks now, it still stole her breath to remember the pain they'd caused her back in Philadelphia. Looking out at the quiet sunlit alley, she sketched *Dead Woman Walking,* a series of panels employing Van Gogh-like distortion in which a woman walked a crowded city, experiencing each passing entity as an onslaught, her sensory portals steadily weakening until finally they were destroyed, and then she stumbled along in total affective darkness, unable to feel at all.

Every afternoon now she and the boy went down to the river, but never once did they see any sign of the bobcat. They searched for her tracks and those of her kittens, but there'd been no rain in a while and the top layer of dirt had turned to a fine dust that was smoothed by the slightest breeze.

Was she waiting for him, Laurelie wondered, *too*?

When finally he came it was late one Saturday evening, without his dog, and long after she'd stopped expecting him. He walked up the trail and then stood at the screen door mouth-breathing, but he wouldn't come in.

"Come out with me," he said.

He took her to the local pub, the place she'd seen him once before. But on this night it wasn't quiet as it had been that weekday afternoon. In the doorway he hesitated, taking in the busy hives of families humming at every table, the bar crowded with leathery men watching car races on the flat-screen TVs. The closest one looked over as they entered and a ripple of heads down the bar followed his. She flushed beneath those gazes, conjoined parts of the same giant face taking in the curves of her body and her freshly brushed hair. Beside her the hiker's face worked hard. She was ready to turn and leave, but he lowered his head and charged in, heading for an empty table in a corner at the back. It was separated from the rest of the room by a no-man's-land scattered with cords and chairs and boxy amps. Next to it a door onto the alley was pushed wide, and a breeze came through.

A waitress came over shortly after they sat down, and Laurelie ordered a ginger ale. The hiker ordered two pints of a local beer, and as soon as the waitress returned with them he drank one until it was empty. He didn't touch the bread she left, just wiped his eyes and drank and panted, his grip on his glass tightening with every chair scrape, every clink of bottle and peal of laughter. The breeze helped, but it could only do so much, for the air was dense with human smells of perfume and sweat and grease. He said nothing; she wasn't sure he was able to.

Soon three musicians came and settled down onto the chairs in front of them. She worried he'd bolt as they began sounding off discordant flurries and strums, but once they rolled together into a loud frolicking Celtic piece, his hands relaxed a little and the frantic pulse of his nose slowed. She imagined the music forming a kind of living barrier, blocking not only all the other sounds, but sights and smells as well.

At the band's first break all the stimuli came rushing back in. They left then, the potency of the crowd pushing on their backs as they hurried out the door. He took a circuitous route home, following back roads, some of which weren't even paved, and rutted tracks so camouflaged that they no longer existed when she turned around. The windows were down and *Congotronics* played and the wind buffeted their faces, warm swells peppered with cold spots she imagined being torn off up in Canada and drifting down. When finally he pulled up to her porch his shoulders were loose and his nose flickered lightly. He sat there a moment, looking out at the night, and then turned to her and smiled.

Think of Gaiman's *The Sandman*, she told herself as they crossed the lane, but once the trail thinned to single file it became a portal to Stephen King. The air was clammy and smelled of wildlife, some of which was no longer living, the slip and crunch of its bones beneath her feet alerting others still very much kicking. A fingernail moon sent down slivers of light but the effect was only disorienting. Large trees seemed to charge at her from the dark, but it was the small ones she feared, aiming their sharp limbs right for her eyes. After she'd stopped multiple times the hiker suggested she hold onto the back of his T-shirt. Thereafter she felt braver, absorbing some of his sure-footedness as she walked in his footsteps. Slowly her memories merged with what she could see, seeping over her line of sight like slow lava and filling in gaps, the granite left by an ancient glacier, the nurse log bursting with pulp, the last curve before the river and then the spongy sloping ground beneath her feet.

The river shone like a slab of obsidian under the weak moonlight. From it came the sounds of splashing, which the hiker said were frogs and trout and turtles and bats, all hunting the insects that fed on the water's surface at night.

Then they were moving again, tramping through ferns that clutched at her legs like sticky hands charged with static. Crossing the needled floor of the pine clearing, the whole forest seemed to hush, and she imagined for a moment she heard druids chanting, far off. Then they were beyond the clearing and moving through the densest section of trees in total darkness, following a path too twisting for her mind to plot until they reached the blackberry thicket that hid his bobcat's den.

They didn't enter this time. The kits are hunting, he said, so they sat down on the forest floor and waited for them. In darkness the silence seemed immense. Without sight or sound it was impossible to gauge whether one minute passed or many before the night exploded. The bob-kittens burst from the brush like the thunder of a hundred bears while all around them a high-pitched keening filled the air, at once animal and resonant with human longing and jealousy and fear. Then it trailed off, and the quiet that remained was full of softly chirping shadows, thumping supple and epiphanic into her lap from the dark, their needle teeth like tiny punishments each time she tried to keep them. They'd grown bigger, but still their mother stayed near, for although Laurelie never saw her, the hiker made a low rumbling sound once, and she answered.

Their steps were fleet as they headed home, and she imagined they were clothed in leaves and skins, plunging and weaving barefoot through the trees.

But in the morning all those images from the night before were as nebulous as her dreams. They smoked and curled, drifting away like ashes when she sat up on the blanket and looked around. They hadn't touched the night before, hadn't touched since the night they'd danced, and now the space next to her was bare. For a moment she felt bereft, believing he'd left while she was sleeping. But then she heard noises from the kitchen and, wandering in, found the hiker there. He was bent over the oven, poking at something that smelled delicious. And seeing him in that position, she suddenly experienced an aching so strong that she had to sit down. She stared down at her table, seeing the whorls of wood not as sources but as sinks, and imagined the hiker's core of energy as like that, never pushing out, only sucking in.

"Who are you," she asked quietly, "when you're not here?"

He closed the oven and turned around, and she didn't need to look up to know his nostrils were flared.

He walked to the sink and turned the faucet on. "I'm a landscaper," he said, and with his back to her his voice was blurred almost to indistinctness amidst the sound of the water.

Now she traced one whorl of wood slowly backward from inside to out. Pictured him as if from a bird's-eye view, a tiny figure toiling in an enormous Eden riotous with insects and flowers and birds. After a while she added rolling lawns and, far in the distance, a mansion. Beside his figure she drew a winding brick path, upon which a woman in a flowing gown approached. She halted beside a rose bed, and as the panel panned in she leaned down to touch one tiny perfect bud. Her fingernails were long and curved, and their color was a perfect match. She looked up at the hiker, and her face was the face of a bobcat.

He went outside for herbs, and she watched him through the screen door cutting sprigs and tasting them. Coming in again, he passed so close she could smell them on his breath. He paused there for just a moment before moving on, but long enough for her to sense his solidness, all the hard long length of him pushing down on the earth, to see the rise and fall of his chest and hear his quickening breath, to feel it stir her hair, and for that one moment it seemed there were no secrets, no barriers between them at all.

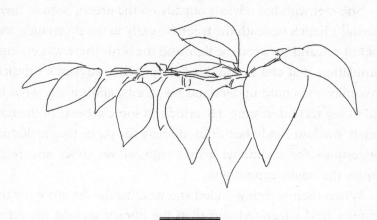

11

Later that moment stretched and grew as gilded as Klimt's *The Kiss*. The summer semester was giving her plenty of other things to do, but she craved those panels like an addict, working on them whenever she could. Dwelling on the hiker's touch was its own palliative to her fear, so she gave her imaginings free rein. And nature conspired with her, for by now capricious spring had morphed into pregnant summer, and the sun bore down all day through diaphanous haze, egging her on. Standing on the trail while the boy hunted for treasure she felt dazzled and addled, dull and maddened by the slow creep of time. She thought about the cold rigidity of isolation, its rationality and reflectiveness undisturbed by urges or recoils, and where once it had felt like safety, now it felt like death.

She met with her advisor outside on the green, both of them sharing a bench beneath the trees. So early in the morning it was not hot yet, and between the light and the birds there was enough stimulation that she found even despite her advisor's physical proximity she could understand his words, and mostly what he had to say was interesting. He criticized some aspects of the new panels she had made but offered ideas for them too, including suggestions for additional artists with whose styles and techniques she might experiment.

When their meeting ended she went to the art store for the supplies he'd suggested and then the library seeking his references, where she settled in with a tall stack of art books to draw through the heat of the day. She used Bonnard for *Pub Chaos*, whose remarkable range of colors and strokes, her advisor had pointed out, made his interior spaces feel so close and intense. The hiker she drew in black and white as ground, but everything else in the pub resounded with the colors of her new pigment sticks, cadmium reds and apricot yellows, sapphire blues and viridian greens, and all those colors were reflected back through his eyes. She used Cezanne's watercolors for *Eden*, trying with translucent washes to make the hiker's garden feel spiritually transcendental while the artist's style of fine pencil lines underneath the washes made feral the expressions on the hiker and bobcat woman's faces.

For the night forest scenes in *Bobcat Nocturne* she experimented with graphite cut through beeswax and then tinted over with colored chalk, the layering process similar to a grisaille and glazing technique, creating a radiance like looking through stained glass. Hot temperatures softened the beeswax and made it easier to blend, and so she was working on these out in her yard when the hiker's truck turned down the lane the following

Saturday afternoon. *Near blue, purple becomes red, and near yellow, green becomes blue,* she thought, and then put down her sketchbook and stepped out from the maple shade into sunlight that struck like a fever.

The hiker got out of his truck. After drawing him so many times she could read the motions of his body like a language. The way his shoulders came forward and his stride extended as he grew nearer, so that it seemed as if he were not walking but gliding, the way his nostrils went from a flicker to a dance and his mouth opened and began panting. And then it all became part of the same fever as he reached her and his hands gripped her and his head bent and hers raised, everything coursing and coming off her in waves as their mouths finally met.

The rowboat looked even older than his truck, strapped to its bed with the gate down and a red rag tied to the end. Its wooden hull was worn to a silky gray and its flat bottom was bare but for a rope and two hard benches. But he pronounced it seaworthy, and after loading it onto a little homemade boat dolly, he handed her a pair of oars from the truck and extracted a small pack from the camping gear in the back, and then they headed down the trail to the river. There he left the dolly and dragged the boat into the water. They boarded on the other side of Thinking Rock and pushed off into the current. Slowly then, the hiker began rowing them upstream. For a long time it seemed as if they were rounding the same bend, its thin spill of shore hemmed in by pines, but finally the land straightened out and the riverbank steepened, and above it the pine clearing appeared. From that distance it glimmered like a jewel, a tiny oval carpeted in orange needles. For an instant she thought she saw the bobcat slinking along its back, but then it was gone, the clearing was behind them, and the river stretched ahead, glossy and endless.

Hardly any time seemed to pass before the hiker aimed back toward the side again, heading for a shady scooped-out hollow. The river was still deep where it met the steep bank of dirt and stone shot through with thick tree roots. One of these arced out over the water and the hiker took hold of it as they approached and tied the boat's bowline to it.

He'd planned this, it seemed, for now he opened his backpack and pulled out a veritable feast. He'd made three different cold salads and each one of them surprised her, for their tastes were at once familiar and unexpected. He smiled at her reactions and his nose seemed to tease, so that after a while she closed her eyes to sharpen her focus and tried to guess their secret ingredients.

"Nuts," she said finally for the potato salad, ignoring the obvious fact that its main ingredient was blue.

"Mm," he said, nodding. "Almond butter, actually."

Fruit salad came next, the fruit finely chopped and drenched in a rich speckled cream. After a few bites she put the container to her nose.

"Christmas," she said, "and flowers."

"Nutmeg. Rosewater." He smiled.

Noodles, finally, shiny and translucent, and all tangled up with slippery green threads. She ate some, poked at it, and then ate some more.

"Licorice . . ."

"Star anise."

". . . and ocean."

"Ha. Dried bonito flakes."

They both laughed then, and she spent the rest of the meal feeling extraordinarily pleased.

Back on the river. Back in the sun. They were sipping from a thermos now, passing it back and forth between them, inside it an icy mango lassi he'd lightly spiked with rum that was without a doubt the best thing she'd ever tasted. The boat moved steadily against the slow current, with a strange effect of relativity as they continued upriver that made it seem they were still and only the scenery moved. She watched it pass, attuned to all the minute rhythms, the tug and glide of the boat through the water and the quiet splash of oars, the hiker leaning toward her and pulling away again, the pulse of his nose and the drop of sweat that slipped from his temple and fell at intervals to the floor of the boat. So lulled was she by these reiterations that she didn't even notice the small dock they were approaching until the motorboat beside it roared to life.

It sped away and then she had to hold on while their own boat bobbed and shuddered in its wake. The hiker said nothing but he stopped rowing, his nostrils white with distaste.

Hardly had they started moving before his nose flared hard again.

"Is it coming back?" she asked, but he only shook his head. They were rounding a wide curve, and his nose was working frantically. Soon she saw why; there were dozens of people in the water just ahead, swimming around a wide dock emblazoned with a large green M. With no more trees intervening, their laughs and shouts carried toward the boat, punctuated by a frenetic pulse of house music. Males cavorted in the water and submerged, diving after footballs or each other, ignoring the rowboat weaving through their midst. Females lay sunning themselves on the dock, and the hiker, trying to avoid the swimmers, rowed the boat so close to them that Laurelie could see their minute changes of expression as they spoke and each adjustment they made to their bodies and hair.

Then the dock was behind them, and the river valley stretched unbroken again. But something lingered, in the water and air. Like the motorboat, the Montague students had left a wake. And yet oddly, though it had shaken her, she did not feel it as a threat, but rather as something almost quaint, a possibility of being that was lost to her now, although not regrettably.

The hiker's eyes, however, were streaming, and his nose still skittered with a hectic beat. He seemed to fight the current now, mouth-breathing with his muscles locked as he dragged them foot by agonizing foot farther up the river. He did not speak and it seemed to her that he wanted to bear his pain privately, so she looked away and pretended not to see, but still it colored everything.

Then he stopped, and settled the oars, and slipped backward into the river. When he surfaced again he was already yards away, flicking the hair from his forehead with a twist of his head and running large brown hands down his face. His expression was calm now, soft. He looked at her, and she thought he was waiting. So she took a deep breath and jumped in.

The cold of the water was heart-stopping, even despite the heat of the air. Surfacing again, she treaded in a slow circle, feeling the current's invisible pull. The dark river was completely empty but for the boat, still rocking, ghostlike, from her exit, even as it too drifted downstream.

He was under there, somewhere. Closing her eyes, she let

herself sink. Her face passed beneath the water two long beats
before her feet hit the bottom. She stayed down, slowly letting
go of her breath until she could take it no longer, and then burst
back into the air and opened her eyes and he was there, inches
from her face.

Their first kiss had been a fever. The second was a cleans-
ing. A kiss blinded by light and with water coursing down their
mouths, his hands on her and his legs brushing through hers, his
skin blessing hers everywhere they touched, filled with an awareness beyond itself, as if part of a far larger embrace between the
river and the sun.

Once out, how did one get back in a rowboat drifting down a
river?

He'd made it look easy, but at the same time unreproducible,
grabbing the rim with both hands and then, in a single fluid
motion her brain captured as a photograph, pulling himself up
and over into the rowboat, arms taut, waist twisting, legs folding
as he dropped out of sight.

Alone then, the river was no longer a caress, but rather a vast
open mouth, swallowing the horizon and the deeply forested
banks. The walls of the rowboat towered above her head. She
peered up at their bowed planks, imagining her skin catching on
fat splinters as she clawed her way over. Then he called out, and
with a deep breath she reached up and took hold of the rim. It
came down fast, dipping so low that some of the river spilled in.
He was helping from above, shifting his weight, first toward her
and then away again. She hooked one knee over the edge, and
then scrabbled the rest of the way in. Once landed, she stayed

down, curled at the bottom studying the grain of the boards, focused on their gentle flexing and the way the hot air above them glittered, and the contrast of their grayness with the pink of her own skin. Once her pulse had slowed, his fingers began gently stroking her hair, trailing softly down the long wet strands.

She might have remained there forever, but for the enormous flying insect that tried to land on her arm. She waved the limb but the insect only banked before resuming fast darts, now at her face. Once more she swung and this time by pure chance crushed its body between her hand and the side of the rowboat.

She sat up then. "I thought," she said, flushing at the smear of wings and entrails, "that it was going to sting me."

She imagined the hiker would be angered by the unnecessary loss of life. But when she looked at him his eyes were half-closed and his nostrils soft, with a lock of her hair still pressed beneath it like a mustache.

"That looks like a proboscis to me," he said.

She scraped the carcass over the side and sat back again, grateful that at least it hadn't been defenseless, but stricken now by the terrible harmony of life having to feed on other life, and so all of it having to feel that pain.

He said nothing else about the insect but after a while started telling her in a quiet voice about weeds. How morning glory would cross half a mile of shade to choke off all of its competitors, how goutweed stayed alive without sunlight for decades and crabgrass could flourish in a thin crack of asphalt and cutting knotweed only made it spread and if you left even an inch of its stalk or root lying around somewhere else in half a season you'd have an acre there.

His hands left her then and pulled a harmonica from his bag, black-toothed and silver-backed, its body rubbed shiny with use. Leaning back, he sounded a few sighs into it and then began to play. Some snatches she recognized, others she did not, one bleeding into the next with no pause between them. He played with his eyes closed and his nose keeping time as the melody surged and trembled and fell. It made her want to move and so she took up the heavy oars and rowed until her arms burned like hot pipes, but it was a good hurt, and a good motion, fusing her to the river and the hiker's music.

The first few spatters of rain startled them both. They stared up into a hazy leaden blue, and then the hiker took the oars back and rowed like it was a race, with his eyes fixed on clouds that came from nowhere and steadily thickened and darkened above. As they passed the barren Montague dock there came a distant rumble of thunder and the boat jerked ahead with renewed speed. She shivered, for without sun the temperature had fallen and the wind was picking up, tousling the water's surface and shaking the trees, asserting its own wild song. Now rain began in earnest, fat drops that smacked noisily against the bottom of the boat and merged into a thudding downpour more solid than particulate, shattering the river into billions of overlapping rings. Then finally they were gliding up to Thinking Rock, and the hiker was steering them around to its shallow side. He let go of the oars, looked down at his hands, and grimaced. But when he looked up at her, he grinned.

A crack split the air over their heads as they dragged the boat from the water. They left it there and ran up the trail with a long brontide of thunder still threatening. When they burst through her door, the boy cat ran down the stairs meowing piteously. The hiker scooped him up and they stood together at the picture window watching the storm toss the forest, waiting for each flash of lightning, so stark in the premature dark, listening in the aftermath of each sonic boom to the soft scratch of the cat's tongue licking the rain from the hiker's skin. And Laurelie imagined it as an ending and a beginning. As if the lightning signaled the end of the world, but at the same time charged them with an infinitely precious substance from which a new one would be born.

That night he reached for her hand as they lay together in the dark, so that his warm fingers were the last thing she felt before falling asleep, and the first thing she felt upon waking. Opening her eyes, seeing his mouth so close, she felt a stab of longing to kiss him. Closing them again, it seemed like a dream when she felt his lips touch hers.

Kissing then. Fingers intertwined. Sunlight creeping over them. Two mouths exploring this new place between them like a forest, acclimating to all its paths and scents and textures. Until her stomach growled, and his answered, and then his lips smiled against hers, and he rose.

Before he left, he checked on the tomato plants. True to his word they hadn't died; in fact they'd grown so large that they sagged now under their own weight. Water too had bent and parted their stems, but otherwise they were unharmed by the deluge of the day before. Dozens of globes hung from the fragrant leaves, ranging from pale green to deepest orange. One fell off into her hand when she touched it, and its fruit was sweeter than candy on her tongue.

The hiker had trotted around to the back of his truck and returned now with two large spirals of metal. Carefully lifting the head of each plant, he slid one of the spirals down over it, and then bent and slowly circled it, threading its branches through the wires with gentle hands.

Watching, she imagined him in his own garden. She pictured a cabin in a sunny clearing surrounded by woods, beside it a small and very neatly tended patch heavy with ripening fruits and vegetables. And it seemed he'd been thinking much the same, because when he rose he brushed his hands on his jeans and, looking down at the ground with his nostrils fluttering, invited her to visit him the next weekend at his home in Maine.

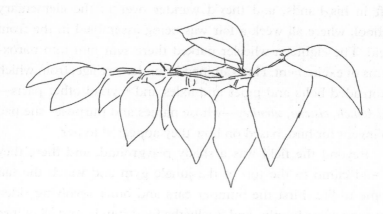

12

Everyone was talking about it, the hottest July on record; she heard the words repeated everywhere she went. She tried to imagine six months of winter and it seemed everyone else was doing the same, because firewood and wood pellets were being delivered to yards and porches all over town. But the concept of cold had no meaning surrounded by so much life, and all those dead piles of potential energy looked vaguely ridiculous, as if the very air forged hotter than they ever might.

Everything was thriving, gorging on life, including the boy she babysat in the afternoons. Daily he devoured her tomato crop, plucking any fruit that was even slightly yellow and popping it into his mouth before she could stop him, until finally some internal limit was reached. Then he'd drop whatever was left in his hands, and they'd wander over to the elementary school, where all week a fair was being assembled in the front field. The eighteen-wheeler parked there sent him into paroxysms of excitement. He examined its undercarriage, from which protruded bolts and pipes and axles and myriad other parts— *sidewinch, cistern, turnkey*—whose names and purposes she had to invent for him, based on how they appeared to her.

Beyond the field was a shady playground, and there they would climb to the top of the jungle gym and watch the fair come to life. First the bumper cars and other revolving rides, then the game booths, and finally the food stands, and all of it so full of promise, coming alive like the most improbable dream.

The physical labor was performed by short dark men, who moved ponderously through the field with the bottoms of their T-shirts folded up, exposing their broad bellies in what seemed, in that sweltering heat, a perfectly appropriate solution. They took breaks in the shade of the playground not far from her and the boy, sitting quietly talking to each other and nodding or smiling whenever she looked their way. The lilting spill of their language transported her and the boy in their play, so that each slide and bridge and ladder became a passage to foreign lands.

Then finally it was Friday, and the fair had opened. But up close the dream shattered, for the cotton candy was melting and the hot dogs were gray, the prizes were dusty and all the rides were old and rusty, and their blaring sound and light displays only made the boy afraid. The white men with prison tats that manned them had a similar effect on her, eyeing her in an overbright way. So she took him away to the air-conditioned bookstore in town, where they played on the model train table for the rest of the day, pretending they were making deliveries to Bar Harbor, Maine.

The bus was crowded despite the hour, having originated in New York City. Laurelie sat next to a woman with a waist-length gun-metal braid who spent the ride glued to a paperback romance, her feet rubbing each other under her seat. The first hour, Laurelie passed staring out at what might have been a single evergreen, looping endlessly. Eventually her nerves settled into a high-pitched hum and she took out her sketchbook and began to draw. *Bus People*, some cocooned in wires and screens, some with eyes that swiveled on stalks, some whose seats had fused to their backs like carapaces. Near Portland, the highway threaded close to the coast, yielding dramatic glimpses of rocky bays. But after Freeport they headed north and west again, back into the trees. At Bangor they turned once more south and east, and then the miles seemed to fly. The land gradually flattened and filled with rivulets, each seeking its own path to the sea. The bus chose one and followed it until it emptied into a wide-mouthed bay, at which point it left the mainland behind entirely, rumbling over a series of high bridges beneath which, in odd reversal, the sea looked like an azure land on which the land lay in emerald lakes.

Stepping off the bus five hours later was a sudden shifting of scenes. The heat wave that was smothering Vermont was gone. Here a salt breeze touched her with clammy fingers that still carried a hint of winter's bone clutch. She shivered, gripping her backpack's straps, wishing, for a moment, that she was home in her cottage. But then the hiker was there, pushing toward her through a crowd of tourists with his dog at his side, its head and tail raised high. The hiker's own jaw was clenched and his eyes were watering and his nostrils were whipping like sheets in the wind, and yet despite this he looked to her to be the most solid thing there, as if the people he passed were only sound and air, while he was rock, country, planet.

He told her he lived south of town on Strawberry Hill, but it rose more like a mountain as they climbed, twisting and turning through miles of forest in which the only evidence of humanity were occasional mailboxes, beyond which driveways led deeper into the trees. At the top of the hill was a gabled house of rough-hewn timber on a small patch of cleared land. When he turned into it she found herself holding her breath, for the scene was so much like what she'd been imagining that she now waited for it to shatter, like the fair had, becoming something she could not anticipate.

She did not have to wait long. As she was climbing down from the truck, the curtains in the front window swayed. A moment later the front door opened and a woman came out. A stranger approaching was a blank canvas, but this woman was already a painting. She walked with the hiker's own panther-like grace. Her hair was the same fathomless black, though it was threaded with gray, and fell heavy and straight to her shoulders with no hint of his rebellious twists and waves. Her face carried his wide gaze as well, but hers was a liquid black, not changing as his did through the forest's hues, and her skin was a darker brown with cool jewel undertones.

Now from the doorway behind the woman emerged the hiker's curls, except blond and on a skin so fair as to appear almost translucent. This man was even taller and sparer of flesh than the hiker, but he bore the same wide frame and long limbs corded with ropy muscle.

All this Laurelie absorbed as the woman came down the front walk. "Welcome," she said upon reaching her, and even her speech was arresting, richly modulated and fluid of tone. She laid light hands on Laurelie's arms and leaned in so that their cheeks barely brushed before pulling away again. "You must be Laurelie," she said.

Afternoon gave way to evening in the hiker's family's kitchen. Modeled after a Spanish hacienda, the floor plan was open and spacious, with cool clay tile floors and stucco walls and a high exposed-beam ceiling. The room overlooked the backyard, and with the large windows open and the patio doors flung wide, letting in the cool salt air, it felt as if they were outside.

Laurelie, to her intense relief, had been stationed at the sink, washing the vegetables for their evening meal. Periodically the mother would call her to the center island, where Laurelie watched her select the next items to be cleaned from two big clay pots on the counter, all freshly picked, she said, from her greenhouse that morning. Standing so close their hips and shoulders brushed, the mother turned each piece in knowing brown fingers, pointing out defects that should be scrubbed or cut away.

In between these conferences, the mother stirred and tasted, all the while discoursing on every manner of thing in a voice that often sounded as if she were singing. The father stood near her chopping things, interacting with her as if his hands were an extension of her own. She told Laurelie he was making the filling for a tourtière, and then explained that this was a famous pastry from his birthplace, a region of Quebec called Saguenay-Lac-Saint-Jean. To which the father added, chuckling quietly, "Beh, zis is basically ze meat pie."

The hiker stood at a countertop across the room making

corn chowder and lobster cakes. Each time Laurelie looked over he was busy at some task, but the lines of his body stayed relaxed. He worked so quietly that sometimes, amid all the stimulation of the mother, she forgot he was there. Other times, hearing his mother's voice shift into some minor key, she'd glance up and catch the woman watching him.

Now the father carried his pan to the stove, and the air filled with sizzling sounds and the heady fragrance of browning meat. "Duck, rabbit, and venison," the mother sang and, scooping a little of the melting fat from his pot, dribbled it into her flour. Motioning with a powdery gesture toward the front door, she added proudly, "My son, he takes them all right here from our own woods."

Takes them, Laurelie thought, *hunts them*, and the very air seemed to charge, grow harsher in some way as the meaning of those words sank in.

The hiker hissed out a breath then. As one they all turned and saw him holding up a hand, and blood tracing down his palm.

Maybe it had taken a while, but she hadn't lost any yolks to the whites, not irretrievably at least. The hiker's mother had tasked her with separating eggs while she'd taken care of the hiker's wound. It hadn't looked deep but still she'd swathed the entire hand in bandages. Then she'd come back and dumped sugar and cream into Laurelie's pot without even measuring. Now Laurelie stirred the mixture at the stove, and it was beginning to thicken and cling. Afraid it would burn, she looked around for help, but the mother and father had their heads together and were assembling the pie in low voices. The hiker was at the stove frying his lobster cakes. There was tension now in his shoulders and hips, in the way he moved his arms. Not wanting to make it worse, Laurelie kept silent and stirred like mad. Finally the mother returned. She'd grown quiet too, nearly brusque as she took the pan from Laurelie. "Rest," she said, pointing to a little bistro table beside which the dog sat with his ears cocked back, staring out the open patio doors.

Shortly thereafter Laurelie was sitting too, charged with nothing more than occasionally turning the handle of an ice cream maker. She could hear the dog breathing, and thought he must be smelling the sea, wondered if he could hear the distant crashing of waves. The air trickling through the patio doors had grown colder as evening set in, far colder than the kitchen now that the oven was on. The mother had it open and was covering the pie; already brown juices were squirting through the crust, and a smell like baking bread wafted past Laurelie as it was pulled out through the doors. The hiker, next to his mother, lifted steaming cakes from his skillet, and although they didn't speak, still it seemed to Laurelie as if their bodies whispered.

With their meal served the mother grew expansive again. She'd set out tall glasses filled to the brim with ice and a ruby liquid and explained to Laurelie while they ate how it was made from a Jamaican flower called sorrel that she grew in her greenhouse. The flowers had to be dried thoroughly upside down, she said, and then steeped overnight with sugar and ginger and cloves before adding dark Jamaican rum.

The food and drink reenergized Laurelie as well, and she

took in the environment with newfound focus as the woman spoke. The father was eating quietly with eyes on his plate, his forehead creasing with deep lines each time he took a bite. The hiker too gazed down at his food, his movements methodical, his nostrils half-flared. Beyond the table, the patio stretched a few more yards in an interlocking pattern of red brick and tiny white stones before giving way to a sloping lawn. The top of the lawn was still dotted with the flowering redbuds of spring, making her imagine that by traveling north she'd also slipped back in time. Halfway down the slope she could see the glass roof of a greenhouse. The edge of the cleared land was not visible from her seat, but beyond and all around it the woods stretched unbroken, steeply descending to a thin stripe of sea.

"—relie?"

In the silence the last few seconds of sound replayed, calling Laurelie back to her place at the table. She swiveled quickly, flushing to realize how far she'd turned her body away. The mother was smiling at her, but it felt hard and careful, and her eyes looked so much like marbles in the fading light that Laurelie had to suppress the urge to shudder.

"Rafe asked what you were studying at Montague."

"Art," said Laurelie, and now the heat of her cheeks was like a brand in the cool evening air.

The father nodded encouragingly, but the mother's eyebrows drew together into two soft puffs Laurelie recognized from the son's own face.

"My son was going to be a doctor"—the mother's eyes tracked now to the hiker's face, and for a moment her voice faltered as they took in its turbulence— "but he chose to become part of our family business instead. He is much like my grandmother, I think." Her voice grew stronger as she continued.

"She started our business, many years ago. She lived far north where there were no white doctors yet, and no white medicines either. She was known for her skill with plants, and so the white harvesters and lumbermen would come to her with their sicknesses, and she would give them the medicines of her people." Now the mother's dark gaze reached for the sea. "The whites called them the Penobscot, but I don't know what they called themselves. If my mother knew, she never told me. They weren't allowed to speak their language, and so my mother spoke only English. But she learned their medicines. My grandmother taught her how to find them in the woods and fields, and to cultivate them in her own garden. Once my grandmother died, my mother continued the business alone. Then she met my father. A Jamaican, he came to Maine as a blueberry harvester during the war. He'd never known such cold! My mother cured his chilblains."

She smiled then. So did the father. Even the hiker seemed to smile, his nose pulsing so slowly that it seemed almost still.

"But he missed the sea, my father did, and so when I was born they moved to Bar Harbor. There were many white people here, but they didn't know how to care for their gardens. So there was much work for us. Too much work, eventually."

The father chuckled then, and said, "Zis is why zey hired me."

Was this really the hiker's room? It looked like a guest room, tucked away between the front door and the stairs. Small and square, its furnishing was spare, with only a desk, a futon and a wall of empty bookshelves. Two other walls were entirely bare, while the fourth consisted of windows facing the road and the forest beyond.

Laurelie could hear the father moving around outside in the hall. She heard him lock the front door and then another quiet click and the stream of light coming from beneath the door disappeared. The stairs creaked as he climbed them, and his footsteps crossed the ceiling above her head. Briefly then she heard muffled voices, the snick of a closing door, and then silence.

No, not silence at all. The hiker brought the forest with him. He came through the door and shut it behind him and opened the windows wide and turned off the lamp. The forest poured in. Crickets and cicadas and frogs, and even once a barred owl. Owls were known for their night vision, he told her, but they also had excellent hearing; those flat faces had feathers that focused sound waves, turning their heads into one great ear. That's why they hooted, to startle prey, for even a shift of a leg or a change of breath could reveal a hiding place. From time to time there came a hoarse screaming, one low and then another higher pitched, which he said were mated foxes seeking each other after hunting alone in the night. They lay on his bed with her hand in his, wrapped together in darkness, listening. It was like sleeping outside, and the air was so crisp she had his down comforter pulled to her chin. But he seemed not to feel it, was lying on top of the covers wearing only his shorts and T-shirt.

After a time she grew warm, and accustomed to the sounds outside, and then she began thinking about the inside again. Though she couldn't see still she turned her head, imagining now that the walls were covered with movie posters and song lyrics scrawled in indelible ink, that there were armless action figures fallen behind the radiator and model cars stuffed inside rows of shoeboxes under the bed. But when she asked about these things he only shook his head. He said that for a long time his room had been upstairs. He'd only moved down here a few years before, because he'd been sick and this room had been easier. That's all he said, and she didn't ask for more, although a thousand questions bloomed in her head. Instead she thought about the panels she'd later make. *Love is a Harmonic,* she'd call it, capturing every detail of lying next to him in that room and on that bed, the gentle pulse of his heart in his hand, the sounds of the night mingling with their breaths.

She felt the mattress stir then as he turned to her. She felt his hand gently moving up her arm. She felt the warmth of his body. *Safe,* she thought, and turned to him, pushing the coverlet to her waist.

There was the hiker, sitting up on the bed, outlined in the flat gray light seeping through the windows. Her eyes drifted closed, and then she opened them again, capturing him in slow snap-shots as he moved toward the door.

The smell of cooking reached her next. Not wanting to be last, she skipped her stretches, but upon reaching the kitchen found she was second. Only the mother was there yet, looking both small and formidable standing at the stove in her long dressing gown, her dark skin high contrast against the white cloth, her spine as straight as a dancer's.

"Good morning, Laurelie. Did you sleep well?" she said.

"Yes, thank you." Laurelie was watching the woman's arm

move, turning slices of meat in a pan. She had an urge to ask if she had slept well too, even though she knew this wouldn't be the right thing to do, knowing moreover that it was only a substitute for other questions she really wanted to ask. And in the silence she began to believe that the mother was having this problem too, that really she'd been asking how the night had passed not just for Laurelie, but between her son and Laurelie. And because neither was able to say what she really meant, both ended up saying nothing more, and as the silence between them grew so did the feeling that if either did speak, nothing they could say would have any meaning at all.

After a while the hiker came in. His hair was damp, fresh from the shower. When he asked Laurelie what she wanted to drink, she saw the mother turn from the stove and take in the distance between them.

He melted chocolate into milk for both of them, then carried their mugs into the dining room. The father soon joined them there with a platter of eggs and Canadian bacon. As they had the night before, the men ate in silence, focused on their food. The mother stayed in the kitchen this time, busy with tasks, passing through only once to snag a few slices of meat and toast before going out again.

After breakfast the hiker's father drove them all down to a harbor in a pickup truck far newer than his son's, where they walked in silence along a dock past a line of boats that seemed to go on forever. There were sailboats, motorboats, houseboats, even luxury crafts. Laurelie read their names to herself as they went, making a note of the cleverest ones, like *Wet Ev Oar* and *Piece of Ship*.

They stopped at a sleek white sailboat called *Minnow*. The others climbed aboard as nimbly as cats, but Laurelie waited until they were occupied before making the leap from swaying dock to rocking hull herself. Once in the boat she sat down on a wooden bench near the wheel. She felt her body sway with the slap of the water against the boat's sides. She listened to the sounds of the mother belowdecks putting things away. She watched the hiker and his father perform myriad tasks with ropes and sails, unfurling some and packing others away and attaching the rest to the boat with knots and pulleys.

Eventually the father came to the wheel and the mother climbed the stairs. They kept their gazes on the sea as the motor rumbled to life and the boat trundled slowly from the dock. The hiker remained on deck and raised the sails. Halfway out of the bay, the wind came up and snapped them tight. The boat cut hard through the water then, and Laurelie's side began to rise. It rose and rose until she was almost standing and had to grip the rail tightly or else fall across the boat and be swept overboard. The danger was real and yet she found if she watched the hiker she felt no fear. His arm was wrapped around the boom and his face was turned into the wind, his mouth open, his eyes wet and fixed upon the waves, his nose pulsing hard.

But as quickly as the wind had risen, so it died. The boat slowed, and then it stopped. The hiker came and sat down beside her. The father sat down beside the mother. Now they drifted directionless on a flat gray sea. The bay was gone, the land but a shadow behind them. Once again the silence grew loud.

Time passed but the scene was so still it could have been a painting. Then abruptly the hiker stood and peered out toward the horizon. His nostrils began flickering erratically, although Laurelie saw nothing where he looked, beyond water and sky. His parents also followed his gaze. The father looked almost like a child with his curls tossed and his eyes expectant and his cheeks still blotchy from the wind. The mother's hair was as smooth as ever, although loosely bound now at the base of her neck. Even as Laurelie regarded her, soft puffs were growing between her brows. And then she smiled.

Now Laurelie saw them too. Dark shapes moving through the water fast, maybe fifty feet off the bow. Then they were arcing through the air, one after another in precise formation. After this impressive display, however, they broke ranks completely, some of the dolphins surrounding the boat, others leading it, some hovering alongside it as if to come along for the ride, some circling it as if to alter its course. And meanwhile they filled the silence with their own private conversation, a strangely intimate mix of clicks and squeals, so that Laurelie imagined they were a bunch of comedians making fun and telling dirty jokes and just generally finding it all hilarious. ,

Then, like the wind, the dolphins departed. Silence returned, but it felt different this time. The sun was high. The air was warm. The sea rocked as gently as a mermaid's bed. The hiker took off his shirt and dove in, and the father was not far behind him. The mother dangled her feet over the side and watched them swim. Laurelie moved to the ladder and incrementally lowered her legs down the rungs. She was wearing a bathing suit under her clothes but did not even consider swimming. Every part that was already submerged felt like one great block of ice. She wondered if she'd even feel it if a fish bit off her toes, and drew them out periodically to take their measure.

When the whale song began she hardly noticed, for it simply added another dimension to the dreamlike intensity of sun and sea. It was the father she noticed first, swimming at a hard crawl back to the boat. He climbed the ladder and then turned with a soft curse in French and regarded the hiker, still some twenty yards out. The mother called out to him but the sound was lost as the whale song swelled, echoing through the water and air, ricocheting up and down the emotional spectrum like some eerily intelligent voice. And the hiker was clearly listening, treading water in a slow circle with his nose pulsing harmony and his eyes wide and weeping, so in thrall to the creature concealed beneath the water that Laurelie imagined he was waiting for it, that it would soon rise from the sea and carry him on its back away from them.

But the whale surfaced behind him. It made a sound like a giant breathing, and then its tubular mass seemed to slide forever across the break it made in the water before its tail rose in the air like an enormous bird, slapped the water's surface once, and disappeared.

The mother went belowdecks after the whale. It was a while before she reemerged, but when she did her smile was back, hard as armor as she passed around plates heavy with tourtière. The father opened a cooler beneath the bench seats and handed out dripping bottles of ginger beer. And now the silence was a veil, shrouding some great mystery whose answer one longed for but would never obtain. Laurelie imagined them as a fresco on the ceiling of some ancient basilica, four pilgrims in a tiny boat atop a flat ocean under a strong sun, partaking of Earth's flesh and blood while one of its great creatures sang. She felt hungry and ate quickly, savoring the marriage of rich meat and salt air in her mouth, not looking up until her plate was empty. The father caught her eye then and nodded.

"La mer," he said, "She brings ze appetite, n'est-ce pas?"

Later the wind picked up again. It pushed them back toward the mouth of the bay, which appeared to be covered in a rippling net. Immediately the hiker rose and began pulling down sails. The father started the motor. Soon the net resolved into birds, careening between sky and sea. As they got closer the engine's noisy putter was drowned out by their screams, and their bodies took on shape and color, gray and sleek and fat with white heads and yellow bills. Before long it grew hard to breathe, for the air stank of fish and something worse—dead fish, on mouths of the birds. Speckled buckshot began striking the deck with ugly smacks.

And then the boat stopped. There was nowhere to go. They were surrounded by the shrieking, jostling birds, who had let the boat into their midst but now would allow them no farther.

"Zey're feasting. Ze tide is slack. We must wait until it turns." Shouting to be heard above the clamor, the father began turning the boat around. But the hiker stood and went to him, and with a murmur took the wheel.

The father stood next to him, both men tall and still, while birds undulated around them like gigantic molecules. The father looked toward the dock, but the hiker looked between the birds and the water. Back and forth, back and forth. Tears beaded in his eyes and fell, and he wiped at them absently with the back of his hand. Then suddenly the boat was moving, sliding into a space that seemed to come into existence even as they entered it. Again the hiker waited, looking back and forth before driving the boat forward once more. In this way, yard by yard, they made slow progress up the bay. Once, as they went on, Laurelie saw a flash of silver in front of the boat rise almost to the water's surface. Hundreds of tiny silver fish formed a sphere that stretched and morphed into a bullet shape before whirling away out of sight. Simultaneously she felt the birds lifting, shifting, and the boat trundled into the space the fish had vacated. Now she thought she understood. The hiker was using the fish to track the path of the birds.

Then finally the birds were behind them, and they were bumping against the dock.

"Mon Dieu," said the father softly.

The mother said nothing at all. Only her hands moved, back and forth, back and forth, smoothing her sundress over her knees.

Upon returning to the hiker's house, Laurelie was ready to rest, wanting nothing more than to lie down and close her eyes for a few minutes. But as soon as they got back, the hiker asked her if she wanted to take a drive. He said he wanted her to see the town before she left, and her bus was leaving too early to save it for the morning.

He seemed excited as they made their way back down the hill, driving fast, squeezing the wheel beneath his hands, a small smile flickering at the corners of his mouth. Once they reached the town, he had to slow. Now they inched down a crowded sunlit hill as a torrent of tourists poured across the road, moving in and out of shops selling everything from African masks and souvenirs to used books and secondhand clothes. A crowd stood outside an ice cream shop. The line was long but no one seemed to mind; those already served lingered in the shade, licking con-tentedly. Laurelie watched them as the truck crept by, finding a surprising comfort in the familiarity of human behavior after her wild day at sea.

The hiker's eyes were watering and his nose was spasming and his knuckles were stretched white over the wheel, but the smile still twitched in the corner of his mouth and his eyebrows were knit into fat satisfied puffs as he drove her through Agamont Park, paused a moment at the Point with its the view of the pier and craggy islands beyond, and, by then panting audibly, exited the town the back way through a bricked maze of alleys full of the clatter of restaurant kitchens and dumpster trash.

He took a winding road away from town and soon made a sharp right onto a wooded track. Now the truck slowed and bumped its way through the forest for nearly an hour, while slowly his face and body relaxed. At the crest of a heavily forested hill, in the middle of a large meadow of waist-high grass, he brought the truck to a halt. Beyond them, as far as the eye could see, stretched a panoramic view of tree-studded islands, sky and sea. Much closer, only a few yards from the windshield, a battered white Sold sign was planted in the ground, looking in that uncultivated place not unlike some ancient explorer's flag.

"It's mine," he said, after a while. "I'm going to build a cabin on it. And I was wondering if you'd want to come and live here with me after you graduate."

Handing around platters of grilled corn and crab, the mother asked Laurelie what she thought of the town, and Laurelie for a panicked instant couldn't remember anything except the hiker's hands in her hair, the bite of the door handle against her back and the slice of sky as he kissed her with the whole length of his body pressed to hers, how the sunlight cut right through the mountain, splashing fire in its haste to reach the sea.

"I was showing her," the hiker said softly, "the place where we're going to live."

To Laurelie then it was like a funhouse mirror, seeing her own emotions twist and distort on the mother's face. For what she felt was the greedy suck of fusion, the breathless passing of a point of no return, and what she saw was the pain and shock of a severed limb. The mother opened her mouth to speak, but then closed it again when the father laid his hand over hers. The hiker and the father began discussing building plans and time-frames and methods for passive energy construction and ways to minimize costs. And Laurelie, listening, thought of the cold sea and the damp breeze and the eight long months of winter.

She startled, flushed, when the mother interrupted, saying, "But what will Laurelie do out there?" And then the hiker turned to look at her, and she knew in another moment he'd perceive how the words laid her own fears bare.

But the father surprised them all. "Beh," he said, "she can draw ze view! And she can work for us also, if she wants to."

The mother stared at him. And then she laughed. The room lit with her laughter, her beautiful mouth parting and her white teeth flashing like flags of truce.

Before the light faded, the mother took Laurelie out to see her greenhouse. Shaped like a pyramid, only its roof was visible from the top of the lawn, its window panels reflecting back the pinks and yellows of the setting sun. Crossing the grass, they passed an old sugar maple. A wire fence beneath it encircled a tidy little house and yard full of chickens. They had long soft feathers sprouting from their heads that made them look like fine ladies wearing fancy hats. She would have liked to stop and watch them stalking around clucking under their breath, but the mother kept going, busy explaining how the father had built the greenhouse right into the southern-facing hill, so that the winter sun would warm it all day while the slope drained away the excess rain and provided shelter from the harsh north winds.

Along the front and sides of the greenhouse lay an enormous outdoor garden. For a moment the mother stopped before the thriving rows of vegetation and fell silent, as if letting them speak for themselves. Soon, however, she resumed walking, but more slowly, leading Laurelie up one row and down the next, both inside the greenhouse and out. She paused at each plant, gently pruned some small fruit or leaf, named it and offered it to Laurelie to taste, and then told her what it needed to grow. There were green beans and lettuce and squash and eggplant and okra and kale and arugula and various peppers and much more, including an entire row of fragrant medicinal herbs growing in such small and delicate arrangements that they resembled clusters of jewels.

While Laurelie appreciated the many names and flavors, understanding the details of each plant's care presupposed far more horticultural knowledge than she possessed, so after a while she gave up trying to absorb all the information. And in fact over time she came to believe that these details weren't even what the mother really wanted to communicate, that actually what she was trying to convey was something larger and deeper about living itself, about how for anything to flourish it had to be given the right environment, and while some things were hardy, others by nature or accident were far more sensitive, and it worked out best when everyone involved was aware of this right from the beginning. Then, upon reaching the end of the last row, the mother said that the father would build Laurelie a greenhouse of her own. At which point Laurelie found herself confessing that she didn't know much about gardening or cooking or building or really anything that involved manipulating physical objects in the real world at all. She expected the mother to be shocked, even contemptuous, but the woman only smiled and gave her a bit of chive flower to taste and told her that sometimes it took many seasons before two plants learned to thrive together in the same ground.

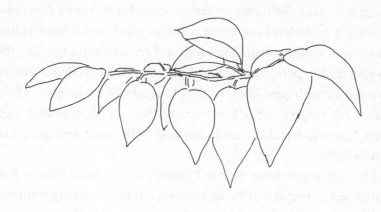

13

Now the heat wave in Vermont subsided. The temperatures were cool again in the mornings and evenings, hot and dry in the afternoons. The hiker arrived each Saturday fairly vibrating after the long drive, full of the energy and excitement of his building plans. Laurelie's own head felt like the sky, huge and blue and dreamy, with emerald hills circling its horizons like promises of things to come. Finally college was almost over; these classes were her last, and moreover all were in some way related to her art. All she had left to do now was to look and draw, and this was exactly what she wanted to do anyway. She looked, she drew. She drew, she looked, images leaping into her mind like chiaroscuro on her bike rides to and from campus and while she was babysitting the boy in the afternoons. Fantastical images, a plant sheltering its fragile child buds from a narcissistic sun; a crowded boat upon a sea of glass and a man riding away from it on a whale that sang; and realistic ones too, like the mother in the park who'd stared off at nothing while her infant tore the air with feral cries, or the old alcoholic in the alley who'd waved his fingers at the boy with a bloom in his eyes and then seen Laurelie watching and dropped both hand and gaze like deadweight.

Nearly a year after fleeing Philadelphia, she still felt the fear portrayed in her art, of being human, a human among humans, as if once rooted it never completely died. But the feeling no longer only made her want to hide. Now she saw how it made her art vital, alive. And with this understanding came another, a sense that she'd been crawling through a passage that was tight and dark and had finally stepped out into light and space.

There came a week when posters blocked her regular view through the windows of the grocery. They plastered the windows of the little pub next door too. WAKE UP, one said, and others said LISTEN and COURAGE and WORLD. The art on them was compelling, blocky and spare, a strong man drumming, a blue horse with wings, a pair of black boots stuffed with stalks of golden wheat. One poster was simply full of art quotes in different fonts and sizes, including Art soothes Pain and Art is the INside of the World. At the bottom of each poster were the coming weekend's dates.

When the hiker hopped down from his truck that Saturday, she asked him if he knew what they were.

"Oh, that's an old New England festival," he said, nodding. "It's held every year out in a fairground in the woods. People go and camp for the weekend. I went a couple of times with my parents, years ago."

"What was it like?" she said.

His gaze blurred, turned inward, remembering. "We saw a puppet show. The puppets were huge." He shrugged. "I was little. But my parents really liked it."

Laurelie nodded. "The posters are amazing. Is it only theater?"

"There was music at night. International stuff. I remember watching some African drumming."

"Wow," she said, and then hesitated. "Were—were there a lot of people?"

Now his eyes focused in on her, so fully she felt pinned. "No," he said, after a moment, "it was pretty small actually."

"They must prefer it that way. I mean, the posters weren't like advertisements. They were like . . . secrets." Her words felt slow coming out beneath the gaze he held trained on her. Fixed. His brow furrowed. His nostrils flared.

It felt as if a spell were cast as they rocketed north on the sun-drenched highway, with verdant hills undulating on every side and Coltrane rocking the cab like a revolution. The hiker drove with one hand on the wheel and the other cupping hers, and she imagined they were soaring high above the world.

When the pickup rumbled to a stop at the end of an exit ramp a few hours later, one enchantment slid seamlessly into the next. Now they rambled along a country road with the windows down and the musky scents of field and forest, the heat-charged air and the green-filtered light, the physicality of all things pressing in.

After a time they came upon a handwritten sign, OXFORD

Fairground 3 Miles. It was stuck in the bare ground with a wooden stake upon which hundreds of little yellow happy face stickers had been affixed. The sign pointed them right onto a rutted track that carved an arc through a field waist-high with wildflowers. Behind the field on one side rose a towering stand of trees. Hemlocks, he told her as they started into the bend, interspersed with red oak and yellow birch.

Almost immediately he slowed. There were vehicles ahead, stopped along both sides of the track. Some of the cars tilted haphazardly down into the tall grass, while others had barely pulled off at all. Laurelie thought at first there'd been an accident, but as their truck crept past, people appeared, some meandering through the field, others lying on hoods looking up at the sky, or sitting hunched in circles in the beds of pickup trucks with smoke drifting white above their heads. Some beckoned or called as they passed. Smiles flashed on and off like fireflies. The hiker's eyes were watering and his nostrils spasmed erratically and his hands were tight on the wheel, but he nodded when she asked if he was okay, and even smiled a little.

Laurelie thought these people seemed strange, but not threatening. *Animal but not predatory*, she thought, *probably because they're all vegetarians.* Then she stared, for ahead the track had straightened out and the scene continued as far as she could see.

They parked in a dirt lot at the end of the track, an impromptu marketplace overflowing with people selling things from the backs of their vehicles. There were blowing bubbles and glow sticks and frayed beach chairs and even piles of old towels and blankets, but apart from tie-dyes and beaded jewelry, Laurelie didn't see anything resembling art. Huge black barrels filled with water lined one edge of the lot, and as they got out of the truck a few dozen shouting people tipped one over.

"Is this . . . ?" Laurelie asked, watching them cavort in the muddy spill.

She didn't finish the sentence, but the hiker shook his head. "Maybe these are just the tailgaters," he said. Then he turned away and pulled his pack from the back of the truck. "Let's find a place to camp."

They followed another hand-lettered sign that read TENT CITY THIS WAY down a wooded path. The sound of music grew steadily louder, until finally the path opened onto a large fairground shaped like a shallow bowl. Its far slopes were swallowed up by forest, but its center was grassy and cleared, although dotted with dancing people now. Many more people were packed around a stage that had been erected at the top of the slope nearest the hiker and Laurelie. The pumping rumba coming from it was deafening as they followed the path behind the stage, and the hiker let go of her hand and covered his ears. Once the stage was behind them, the path traversed another section of trees before reaching a second, smaller clearing. This one was littered with tents and backpacks, but the hiker kept going, heading for the forest on the other side. Soon trees blocked the tents behind them from view. The canopy closed above their heads, making it dark and cool, almost cold without the sun as they made their way down a steep slope to a stream and up again on the other side. Beneath their feet rustled dry needles and leaves, but there was little low growth apart from sporadic clumps of ferns nestled in the thin beams of particle-filled light that escaped the tall trees, and this made it easy to walk along, even though they followed no path.

When the hiker stopped, the only evidence of the festival behind them was a faint thudding sound. He unpacked his tent, and after erecting it on a level patch of ground, unzipped the sleeping sacks and laid them out inside it. Then he pulled a small pack from the larger one and lifted it onto his back.

The crowd around the stage had grown even larger by the time they returned to it. The hiker turned away from it and, skirting the trees, circled around the top edge of the bowl until he reached its far side. There, with deep forest at his back, he sat. Reaching into his pack, he brought out a bottle of mead, snapped off the cap with a hard flick of his thumb, and drank until it was empty.

The sun set slowly behind the trees, the sky in front of them deepening through shades of blue as the night crept in and blotted out the spectacle below. After the Latin band there'd been some kind of electric raga fusion, and now a Québécois folk band played so fast Laurelie's tapping feet could barely keep up with their blurred four-beat rhythm. The crowd of dancers was fading into darkness, and she was sorry to see them go; from her high viewpoint there seemed such an abandon to their bodies, as if the music were a physical substance filling those vessels and setting them in motion.

But darker is better, she thought. The hiker's muscles loosened where their shoulders touched. He had closed his eyes, and now she closed hers too. Felt the mead moving through her blood, the music throbbing in her bones, and the tiny flutters around the area of her heart that happened whenever he was near.

She felt him stiffen and opened her eyes to find a pair of

large brown ones peering at them. They were hung in a pale moon face whose every feature was stamped by the sun with its own set of contour lines, all of it framed like a buffalo head with shaggy blond dreads.

"Man, I thought . . . I was . . . hallucinating you . . ." The words were croaked out on a pent-up breath, a trickle of smoke punctuating each pause; from one weathered hand dangled a smoldering cigar.

Maybe you are, Laurelie thought, for an instant perceiving this strange creature as birthed from this animal place, possessing a connection to it she'd never share. She looked at the hiker then, at the tears beading in the corners of his eyes and the hard flared nostrils and parted panting mouth, and perceived in him an even stronger repulsion to it, but equally one she couldn't share.

Then the light was gone and the music was a throbbing blindness of sinuous beats, the bodies below them a single black mass writhing and pulsating beneath it. Occasionally other bodies passed around them, leaving messy, pungent trails. Hours of steadily sipping mead had made the ground into a sea, the hiker beside her a buoy she gripped lest the waves of input carry her away. She wished they would slow for a moment so she could parse them, but instead they only washed up the walls of her mind and then lurched back again, creating a kind of feedback loop that didn't clarify anything. She thought of the hiker's pulsing nose and weeping eyes and wondered if this were how he always felt, but even as she grasped it the thought slipped back into the waves again.

When finally they could take no more, the hiker led them back to their camp. The tent city had come alive in the darkness; it was a burning city now, with fires flaming all over the ground and candles set high seeming to float in midair and shadows moving all around trailing thin streamers of light. The voices she heard seemed to make no sense, and she imagined this was Babel, a thousand bodies living together and none of them able to communicate.

Back at their own tent, familiar and warm, she lay down upon the furs and immediately sank into the soft folds of sleep. But the hiker pressed her up again, urged her to eat. The meal was tactile in the dark, and she ate hungrily, hunks of dark homemade bread the hiker handed her layered with his rich strong cheese, and every bite washed down with cool water. She ate until the food was gone and then lay down again, only to find herself wide awake.

Drowning no longer, floating now atop the lingering effects of the mead, senses reading loud and clear, mind as expansive as the night. Next to her the hiker's warm body, gently breathing. Searching the darkness for a seam, imagining she was a butterfly in a cocoon, a flower in a seed about to burst. Turning and finding his mouth, finding in it the same readiness. Bodies pressing then, hands tugging at clothes, his hardness slow-fusing with her softness, so that what came next would simply complete a transformation already begun.

Then abruptly he sat up. She couldn't see and so when he didn't speak she tried to imagine what he might be doing. She pictured his ears, swiveling in the dark like a cat's. Once her own breathing slowed, she heard him panting.

"What is it?"

"People." His throat clicked audibly. "They're trying to be

quiet, like they're doing something wrong. And that's how they smell too."

"Outside? How many are there?" Now she sat up and rubbed her fists against her eyes in a useless attempt to see.

"Five guys and one girl."

"Just one girl?"

There were long blank moments in her brain as she crept through the forest, gripping the back of the hiker's T-shirt. Then fear would rush in, huge and cold and real, and for a moment only her blindness stopped her from running. He was moving so slowly, silently and tactically, stopping every few step to smell and listen. He only wanted to know what they were doing out here, and that's why he was taking such pains to remain concealed. But she kept thinking about the girl, where they were taking her, and what they would do to her. He'd said that they were wasted, and that she was too. Had they taken her against her will? Was her own fear rising like flood water as she realized what was happening to her?

Suddenly the hiker made a noise low in his throat and stopped. Out of nothing a tent appeared. A large blue dome, it loomed against the night, flashlight beams canted haphazardly along its walls, casting eerie streaks of light.

Already he was backing away, with no intention of revealing himself now that the threat had been located. But Laurelie stood frozen by the male voices coming from inside. Her heart lost its beat, fluttered and then pounded. Her breath caught in her throat, choking her.

When her fingers dropped from his shirt, the hiker turned

back. His eyes watered freely and his nose pulsed hectically, but his physical reactions didn't restore her; rather they only served to magnify her own.

Then came a feeble moan from inside the tent, unmistakably female, and it was as if the sound propelled her, for she lurched forward, body quaking, hands scrabbling at the door. She tugged up the zipper so that the flap gaped wide, and stumbled inside.

She registered heat, and sweat, and the detritus of men. A thousand yards of blue floor stretched ahead. At its far end were demons. Massive in the stilted light, they huddled in an inverted star around the slumped body of a girl.

Their heads were down, resting or conferring, so that they didn't see Laurelie crawling toward them over the dirty plastic floor, past crumpled beer cans and empty cigarette packs and discarded articles of clothing. But when she reached the closest one, it came alive. She heard its low grunt and smelled its stench and time seemed to slow as all reason fled, stretching like taffy as it lifted its head and fixed its gaze upon her.

A high-pitched cry rent the air then. A bobcat's cry of warning, and longing, and fear. Time snapped, then raced and rippled as all the demons swung their heads, trying to locate the source of the animal sound. Laurelie reached into their midst, grabbed the girl's arm, and pulled hard.

The girl had looked broken, slumped over her knees, but she roused now and slapped Laurelie's hand away. "What the hell are you doing?" she cried.

And now Laurelie saw the needle in her fingers, the drugged bliss on her face, the beaded bag open upon her lap with the lighter and spoon spilling out. The other needles scattered around the floor.

Laurelie looked back and saw the hiker crouching just outside the tent door. His face was a twisting rictus in the slanted
light, and something, sweat or mucus or tears, dripped steadily
from it onto the ground. Beside her she felt more than saw a
demon shift, and then she was moving, exploding out the door
and into the night, with a thousand demons reaching out to keep
her.

They both ran, zigging and zagging through a black maze of
trees until they could run no more. The hiker dropped to his
knees then, panting, and she sank to the ground behind him,
taking great breaths, her pulse slamming in her temples while
her heart in her chest spun and crashed and wheeled.

Adrenaline bled quickly, a mortal wound. Somehow, the hiker
led them back to their tent. Laurelie was shivering by the time
they reached it. Inside, she burrowed deep between the fur-lined
sleeping sacks and stared up at the dark walls of a prison. Eyes
open or closed, it didn't matter. The inverted star hung indelible.
The bobcat's cry echoed in her head. And in the mud of memory her own demon fed, and she heard its grunts and smelled its
firewater breath, felt the brush of its whiskers and the beady
hardness of its gaze.

But these projections were pierced by the hiker's ragged
breathing from the darkness next to her. *Because he'd know*, she
thought, *if a demon were really here. He'd smell it, and hear it, and
taste it.* And now hers faded, and the black walls of the tent
became just walls once more, simply a way for him to keep out
weather and bugs, while blocking nothing of his perceptions. '

"I'm sorry," she said, finally, softly.

His breath hitched, and then he released it, long and slow.
His fingers, beneath the furs, found hers. "It's okay," he said.

In the dawn the air was glittering, white-bright and stifling, and
smelling like bees. The hiker packed the tent away and then all
that remained of the night before were four tiny holes where its
stakes had pierced the ground. In the tent city shadowy indeter-
minate shapes rose and fell behind synthetic walls and the
sounds and scents of partying still came from fire circles, but
the stage as they passed it was dark and deserted, and nothing
moved in the lot where they retrieved the truck. Beer cans led
like crumbs back to the country road where yellow happy face
stickers winked and curled in the dust.

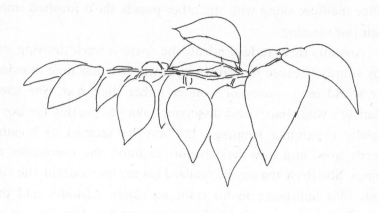

14

Laurelie spent two weeks on *Demons*, studying De Kooning's women and then drawing her rapist like them, five different versions of him all hulking and wild-eyed, with threatening stares and ferocious grins, blending archetypes from cave men to porn stars to slick Wall Street brokers. The hiker she drew as half-bobcat, half-man. In her panels he terrified the demons with his scream, shattering the inverted star they had formed around their prey, and then carried her from their lair and bounded away on all fours with her through a black maze of forest.

Finishing those panels was like waking feverish in the night and kicking away all the covers, only to later freeze and regret it. For late Sunday evening after putting away her oil sticks, she got on her bike and rode to campus, leaving *Demons* in her advisor's office mailbox along with the other panels she'd finished since their last meeting.

Anxious then, indeed adrift, she spent a week drawing the boy simply because he was there. It was her first time drawing the world as a source of wonder rather than fear. She used Matisse's wild shapes and dissonant colors to portray the boy's rapidly expanding language, the way he seemed to breathe words now, and how he'd begun to intuit the ontologies of things. She drew the day he realized his toy trains drank the viscous blue substance in his train set tower. *Liquids!*, said the thought bubble over his head, and surrounding him were more thought bubbles full of diesel and milk, hot chocolate and rivers and rain. She drew the game it became then, of him associating every object with its hypernym, and refining both as new instances were encountered. So boulders became giant rocks, and sugar and salt became sweet and bitter rocks, and at the river there were skip rocks and splash rocks and boom rocks and tinkle rocks, although he didn't know until he threw them in the water which ones they would actually be.

Wednesday he discovered a pile of scat while they were walking along the trail, and once he understood what kind of rocks those little dried lumps were, he was unceasing in his search for further exemplars, discovering as the days went by half a dozen more, not only on the trail but also scattered up and down the thick brushy edge of the dirt lane.

Then came Friday and she sat once more on a hard wooden chair in her advisor's office, staring down at her knotted hands while he stood behind his desk, coffee in hand, slowly turning the stiff creamy pages of her panels and rattling off their titles under his breath. "*Demons, The Storm, Cutting the Roots, Whale Rider, Bobcat Nocturne, Dead Man Walking . . .*"

When he was through he gathered them up again and told her how pleased he was with all she'd accomplished in the three terms since she'd come to Montague. He and his colleagues hadn't been sure how well she'd do, he said, changing colleges so close to graduation.

"I took the liberty of sharing these with them, and we've all agreed," he continued, carrying them over to the couch. He sank down with a sigh, sending fine particles streaming up into the morning light. "We think you're developing an interesting approach, between your sampling of masters and your collage of high and low art forms. We'd like to offer you a place in our graduate program this fall. It will give you time and space to pursue your ideas further. And it will keep you here with us a little while longer, as well."

With a sensation akin to hallucination, she watched his lips stretch over his small yellow teeth and the beveled gray bristles around his mouth rise and fall, as he explained that her tuition would be paid by the department, that she'd have some departmental duties each year, but he thought it would good for her to get some teaching experience, maybe edit the department's art journal, both of which would help bring her out of her shell and get her interacting more with the other art students and faculty. "We want you to feel like you're part of a family here," he said, and then leaned forward, laid her portfolio on the low glass coffee table, and smiled.

On the one hand, there was her future, a black box, its form and function undefined. On the other there was her bike, with its handlebars and seat, its pedals and wheels, the purpose of each so perfectly described. She was atop it now, gathering speed down the hill, laughing aloud with the joy of it, the wind taking it and whirling it around. Fraternity houses flashed past on both sides, and she imagined they were artists' gables, the artists inside dusted with charcoal dust, the tables piled high with brushes and paints and bottles of rabbit skin glue. Then the road leveled out and she passed the meadow and it was full of butterflies. And it seemed to her as if they were all lighter than air, balancing on the forward edge of time.

When the hiker arrived that Saturday, she took him down for a look at the scat the boy had found. To her relief he said they weren't from a bobcat. They came from a dog, he said, probably one that had been abandoned by someone who either didn't know or care that a domesticated animal wouldn't survive in the wild any longer than most people.

Then they climbed into his pickup truck and headed out on another road trip. The last time, driving to the festival, she'd imagined they were flying. But they'd fallen now, and sped low over sun-scorched earth. She gripped the cracked leather edge of the pickup's bucket seat, hearing her breath in her ears and her heart pumping the blood inside her veins, and all the thoughts she held inside made her feel like life was reckless and at any moment something might change, so that all she could do was hold on tight.

If the hiker sensed something unusual, his face didn't show it. For the moment at least, the whirlpool inside her was attributed to the task at hand. They were driving south two hours to her landlords' new beach house, where they would spend the evening babysitting the boy while his parents went out for the evening. Laurelie's landlady had basically forced her into it, accusing her of contract infraction and ingratitude when she'd said she already plans, then threatening her with eviction if she did not comply, and finally begging brazenly, saying she knew very well what Laurelie's plans were, and that her boyfriend could come with her.

The hiker didn't seem to mind as much as Laurelie did. He talked as he drove of poured foundations and roof trusses for the cabin he was building in the woods five hours north. He still thought she was going to come and live there with him once the summer term was over. And of course she still wanted to. The problem was that she wanted two things now. She wanted to live with him. But despite the demons that resided there, she wanted to live in the world too. She wanted to go to graduate school.

High dunes separated the island from the sea. Miles of marsh dotted with birds and the odd fisherman connected it to the mainland. The hiker followed the main island road through a simple grid of numbered streets until they found the right one. They parked in the sandy driveway and then walked around an ultra-modern cape to a deck in back. Laurelie's landlords were waiting for them there, looking out of place in their evening clothes against the casual backdrop of sand.

"Now see, Violet, they aren't late," the landlord said.

The boy was down among the dunes, splashing around in a plastic kiddie pool. When he saw the hiker and Laurelie, he tumbled out and launched himself in their direction. The hiker picked him up and listened to his chatter while the landlady showed Laurelie around the house. Resentment still arced off the woman like sparks, and moreover the walls were laden with her heavy-handed landscapes. Laurelie kept her gaze out the windows. The little cape offered near-panoramic views, each a slightly different perspective on three simple horizontal stripes of sand, sea, and sky vibrating like a Rothko painting.

Down on the deck the three humans were their own study in contrasts, the landlord short and stocky and composed of the same colors as the view, the hiker tall and thin and of tones recalling earth and wood and blood. The boy clung to his shoulder like a little crab, soft and round and pink. As Laurelie watched, the landlord said something and rubbed his pale palms together. The hiker replied with a single word and then turned the boy into an airplane and walked away, flying him around the deck.

By the time Laurelie came outside again the hiker had put the boy down and was out among the low dunes close to the house, bending over an enormous plant with spiky, gray-green leaves. Purple flowered stalks grew from it like giant spears of rock candy. He brushed them gently with his hand and a dozen fat bumblebees wobbled into the air, bumping his head and shoulders in a slow inquisitive dance before settling back down to their flowers. From the deck, the boy stared open-mouthed.

"He said he's from Maine. Whereabouts exactly?" The landlord spoke from an Adirondack chair to one side of the door, startling Laurelie as she came out because she hadn't seen him there.

Laurelie didn't respond. The hiker was crouching now, digging away a bit of sand at the base of the plant, his nostrils pulsing gently.

"Zzzzzzz." The boy buzzed over to her, doing a private little dance of his own.

"Well, in any event, that must be quite a long drive," the landlord continued. "Violet tells me he's been doing it every weekend." He paused and then went on, "And I suppose it'll only continue, now that you'll be staying here for graduate school."

The hiker's face froze, and so, for a moment, did Laurelie's heart.

"You're surprised we knew?" the landlady said, coming through the door. She smiled at the expression on Laurelie's face. "Owen *is* the provost at Montague. You'll need to let us know soon if you're planning to keep the cottage," she went on. "I had someone calling about it just the other day. Oh, and we may need to charge more, if there's going to be two of you."

Behind them the hiker was moving away. Laurelie's pulse fluttered with frantic wing beats as her eyes tracked him heading deeper into the dunes. She was certain he'd heard and yet absurdly still hoped he hadn't and searched for signs of confirmation in the set of his shoulders and length of his stride as her landlords gathered their things and air-kissed the boy and then swept out of the driveway and down the road, waving gaily from their red convertible.

Once they'd gone she felt the emptiness they'd left behind like a vacuum. Into it the gulls screamed. There was a chill dampness to the air, rising from the sand now that the sun was sinking. The hiker looked small wandering out among the swells.

The boy ran after him, and Laurelie watched, hardly breathing, nearly weeping when the hiker stopped and turned and bent down to him. And when the boy ran back to her with joy in his face it seemed as if he were pulling the entire horizon with him, for the hiker was returning too.

They took the boy down to the beach. Laurelie went inside first for snacks and towels, and when she came out again, she found them standing before the open bed of the hiker's pickup truck. She kept some distance between them, but was still close enough to see that his nose flickered erratically and his eyes were damp. Intent as a surgeon, he was weighing a fishing rod in each hand. The boy stood wide-eyed before an array of brightly colored lures the hiker had made of wood and fur and glass; they looked like children's toys but for the medieval-looking hooks protruding from their sides. After a time, the hiker set the longer rod aside. He gathered a few lures into a bag, which he then tied at his waist.

They walked over the dunes, the hiker leading the way with the boy leaping between them, effervescent, crashing into her legs and kicking up great tufts of sand. Down by the sea the sun was low but still heavy and hot, and the air shimmered with reflected heat. It was high tide so she clustered their things on the thin strip of dry sand between the dunes and the water line. The boy ran down to the water's edge and inspected the treasures deposited there by the foamy fingers of the waves. The hiker stood a few yards away looking out at the ocean, his rod held loosely in his hand. When finally he began stringing it, the boy jumped up, eager to assist, and received charge of the bag of lures. The first one the hiker asked him for was a tiny thing with a preponderance of silky black hair. "It'll hover on top of the water like a bug," he told the boy. The next one he requested was a smooth piece of dark wood nearly the length of a butter knife, a thing of beauty with large round eyes and a finely striped and streamlined body that flared out at one end into a wide red circle of mouth. It would glide beneath the water, mimicking the movements of a fish. "The lures I make are like desires," he said, "more tempting even than the real thing." He strung both of them, staggering their lines, to make it seem like a pursuit, he said, because sometimes one's desire could be enhanced by another's. It was the most he had spoken since the landlords left, and though the boy listened raptly, Laurelie felt unbalanced, even a little deranged by the coldly calculating words.

But she missed them once they stopped and the hiker began to cast. He caught nothing there, and after a while the boy lost interest in watching him. He and Laurelie began building a sand train. Slowly the hiker drifted away down the beach, still casting and reeling lazily. Laurelie felt the separation like a physical pain, and believed he intended her to. But once the train was finished, the boy noticed him gone and followed him. And so up the beach they all went, heading for a breakwater of rocks that jutted out to sea in the distance, the hiker casting and reeling down at the water's edge while Laurelie sifted through the powdery sand high up against the dunes. The boy raced ahead and carved circles back, his little legs pumping as he chased seagulls. The birds had no fear of him, even seemed to tease, lifting away like indulgent siblings when he was close enough to grasp their tail feathers, only to land again with a ruffle of wings a short distance behind him.

When they reached the jetty the boy clambered up onto the black rocks with Laurelie close behind. The hiker sloshed out into the water beside them until his calves were submerged, and then he cast.

Hardly a minute passed before he was backing out again, reeling fast, his line whipping and blurring as he dragged a slim silvery fish from the dark sea. It arched and gaped there on the sand, bleeding water. The hiker anchored it with his foot and slid his buck knife through its head just above the eye. Then he removed the hook from its mouth. The small furry lure was still attached. He slid the knife up the fish's belly and swirled both in the water. When they were clean he packed the empty cavity with handfuls of moss he took from his lure bag, then wrapped the whole thing tightly in a cloth and stored it in the same bag.

Now he restrung the small lure in front of the large one and cast again. He went deeper; the low swells of waves had reached his thighs when something took his line. The thin cord buzzed and flew, nearly emptying his spindle before he was able to start drawing it back again. No quick capture this time; it was a battle, soundless and protracted, his pole bending radically as he gave and took slack, Laurelie thinking at any second the metal had to snap. A passing pair of beachcombers stopped to watch, and then another, as the hiker fought to keep his catch.

Slowly it became clear that the pole was bending a little less, the line coming in a little more with each reel, and then it seemed to Laurelie as if all the watchers gave a collective sigh. There were flashes of silver in the shallow and then it was over. The fish was enormous, head to tail the same size as the boy. Everyone but the hiker took a step back as the heavy body flip-flopped on the sand. The hiker anchored its head and extracted the hook. The small lure still dangled sodden from the filament, but the big lure was gone.

The small crowd murmured and gasped when the hiker grasped the fish by both gills and dragged it back into the water. It lay still on the sand beneath the lapping waves for a few long beats, and then drifted off with feeble flicks of its tail, as stunned as the humans watching it leave.

"That would've fed me for a month," one man remarked.

The hiker shook his head. "You can't keep the females."

Back at the beach house the hiker scraped the first fish he'd caught clean of scales on the driveway and then gutted it. The boy crouched next to him and helped him hold the hose, washing away all traces of blood. Then the hiker brought the fish inside and pan-fried it on the stove with the windows wide, sipping homemade beer while the boy pinched salt for him and ground the pepper mill. The boy even tried a bite when the fish was ready, before tucking into the noodles Laurelie had made him.

Afterward they sat on the couch watching a Marlon Brando movie on the old movie channel with the boy snuggled down in the middle, his body a bridge between them, draped over them both, hot and soft and dense. He soon nodded off but they left him there until his parents' headlights turned down the road. Then the hiker carried him off to bed while Laurelie gathered up their belongings.

The night was quiet as they left.

"Want to take a walk?" the hiker said.

They crossed through the dunes and slid down their cool slipping backs onto the beach. It was still and black. The tide was low, the crash of the waves sudden and loud. They walked along the cold hard sand at the water's edge. Above them wheeled an enormous night, its motion like a flower opening, only perceptible once one had looked away for a long time. And so too did she begin slowly but inexorably trying to convince him of how it could still work, and how much she still wanted it to. Living with him on weekends and vacations, both of them working hard when they were apart so that they wouldn't have to while they were together, and she'd take the bus so that he didn't have to drive so much, and did he know that she was very productive in small spaces . . .

And after a while his mouth quieted hers, and then bound together like a raft, they headed back, pitching between the thunder of the waves and the pull of a million stars.

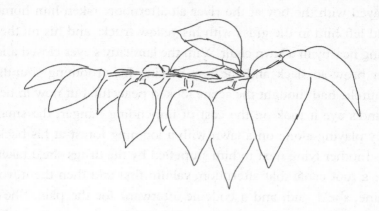

15

"Pick up. Pick up pick up pick up . . ."

She paced the floor of her cottage with her phone to her ear, casting anxious glances out the kitchen window. Signs of fall had cropped up overnight. The bushes bordering the dirt lane were festooned with bright red berries. Shadows were twice the size of their sources although it was only six o'clock, and the cicadas with their steely screech were already calling down the night. She imagined the boy huddled beneath a berry bush somewhere, afraid of the shadows and the sounds of the coming dark. She imagined him plucking a bright red fruit and then lying unconscious in a pool of vomit, with berry-stained lips.

Finally the hiker answered his phone. "He's lost," she blurted, and then he made her back up and explain how she'd played with the boy at the river all afternoon, taken him home and left him in the grass with his yellow trucks and his mother lying nearby in a lawn chair. With the landlady's eyes closed and her brow so slack and the boy making his vrooming sounds, Laurelie had thought the scene looked peaceful, but now in her mind's eye it took on the cast of impending danger, the small boy playing alone on a lawn with a looming forest at his back, his mother lying next to him stupefied by the drugs she'd taken for a root canal that afternoon, valium first and then the novocaine, she'd said, and a codeine afterward for the pain. She'd told Laurelie she must have nodded off, because when she opened her eyes next the boy was gone.

The hiker asked how long. An hour, Laurelie told him, no more. For that's how long ago she'd left them there, and her landlady had only just now knocked on her door, hoping the boy had come to her. "And the worst part," Laurelie said, "is that he probably did, but I wasn't there." The crisp yellow light had drawn her out; she'd been riding her bike north along the river road, sucking stones like Molloy and dreaming of the future to come. Guilt flooded her now and she began pacing again, imagining where the boy might have gone.

"Do you think," she said, "the bobcat . . . ?"

She heard rustling noises, the tug of a zipper, the snick of a door opening and closing and footsteps crunching over gravel. Another door, and then an engine rumbled.

"I'm coming," the hiker said.

Laurelie helped her landlady search the main house first. Then they worked their way slowly down the long hill in the fading light, calling the boy's name with artificial cheer whose only effect was to increase their own anxiety. It was full dark by the time they finished at Laurelie's cottage and thumped back out to stand in stunned silence on her porch.

Only one place left to look. Standing there, Laurelie pictured it. The boy, upon not finding her home, going down the trail to the river where they'd spent the afternoon. *But what then*, she wondered. *How much farther would he have gone?*

Bobcats hunted at dusk. She'd read they could take down prey twice their size. Ice slid down her back at the thought of what one could do to a little boy.

She heard the sound of a car and swung around just in time to see headlights from the river road turning onto the lane. Her heart leapt, though she knew it was too soon.

"That's Owen," her landlady said, and started down the stairs. "I just know he's going to want to call the police."

"Sparkle rocks," Laurelie called out over a pulsing chorus of frogs and cicadas. They sounded so much louder when one was alone and in the dark. She wondered if the boy thought so too. Branches caught at her hair and clothes and protruding roots threatened to derail her but she kept on, heading down the river trail with only a small flashlight to guide her way. She went through flat rocks and finger rocks, smooth rocks and bumpy rocks, crystal rocks and mossy rocks too, focusing fiercely on playing the boy's game until her sandals slapped water, and then she just called his name.

She splashed and slipped across the shallow river to Thinking Rock and then, scrambling up, began scanning the banks, marking a grid with rocks and branches and illuminating every square inch in between, her heart going staccato and her mind filling the grainy dark with images of the little boy's body broken or bitten or trailing pale into the cold black water. And once she'd searched as far as her light could reach, she started all over again.

The rock dug into her tailbone as she slid down from it, and the cold water washed through her shoes. Low-hearted, she sloshed back to the bank, and there shined her light over the ferns. They looked like an ocean in the dark. Behind them rose the forest. Its depths seemed infinite, and yet not far within lay the clearing where the hiker had camped for weeks. The boy might remember the way. There would have still been light when he went in. Now, weaving through the ferns and the trees beyond, she followed no path but the one in her head, heard nothing but her heart and her own fast breaths until finally she emerged onto the clearing.

Running then, she swept her light in great swaths, calling to the boy in a voice pitched low and urgently. When he did not answer, she stood in the center and turned slow circles, incrementally widening the angle of her light until it struck the trees on the clearing's far side.

Somewhere inside them hid the bobcat's den. Would the boy remember how to get there? He had loved the bob-kittens. Would he have gone alone in search of them? And what would the bobcat do to him, without the hiker there?

She had to go in there and look for him, but she was afraid, seemed to feel the bobcat just beyond the reach of her light, warning her to keep away. The minutes ticked by as in her mind grew a sinuous mass, a monstrous bramble patch that defended a bobcat's den, each branch alive and as deadly as the hairs on Medusa's head.

She heard something else breathing behind her. Spinning around, her flashlight beam caught the hiker running toward her across the clearing.

"I just know he's here," she said.

He nodded. Accustomed to the night, his eyes watered at her light, and so she aimed it at the ground as they started off again. But instead of heading for the den he turned back the way they'd come. He strode so quickly through the dark she had trouble following even holding onto his shirt, telling her agitatedly as they went how the landlord had been standing with the police in the lane when he drove in. They'd stopped him and wanted to know what he was doing there, and when he told them, the landlord had decided to go with him, saying he would direct their search at the river while the police handled the second search of the house and grounds.

The landlord had gone to get his car first, in case the boy had been injured. Lights blinded them as they rounded the last bend in the trail, causing the hiker to stop and cover his eyes with his hands. Her landlord had driven in as far as he could and left the high beams on. They were huge and stunningly blue-bright, yet little more effective than Laurelie's own small flashlight at penetrating the night forest.

The man emerged from the front seat. He stepped gingerly down the trail, still wearing his suit and tasseled loafers. Ignoring Laurelie, he handed the hiker a flashlight as big as a car battery, twin to the one in his other hand.

"A boy that small couldn't have gotten far," he said, then

began sweeping his light back and forth across the trail and into the forest on one side, instructing the hiker to do the same on the other.

They crept along at a snail's pace. The hiker's frustration was plain on his face, but he said nothing until they reached the river. There he broke away like he'd been torn and headed into the ferns. Laurelie followed him, but the landlord stopped and stood scanning the river banks, his light bobbing futilely over black water and countless amorphous shapes on the other side. Then, turning around, he shined his light at the hiker, who had just reached the trees. "I don't think he would've gone in there," he called. "In fact, I doubt he even got this far."

When no one replied, he took a few steps into the ferns. The sticky plants clung to his pant legs and draped the ground in layers, making it impossible to see what lay beneath even when directly illuminated. He bent and peered under a dozen stalks before rising with a snort of frustration. "This is ridiculous!" he called. "He could be anywhere in here."

"No," the hiker said, and now his own frustration rang clear. "He left a trail, and I'm following it." He had turned his own light off but even in the weak reflection of Laurelie's own she could see his eyes were streaming and his nostrils were pulsing hard.

For an instant the landlord trained his light directly on the hiker's face. Then he lowered it to the hiker's legs where they disappeared behind the feathery fronds some twenty yards away. "I don't see any trail," he said.

Without a word the hiker turned and started into the trees. He seemed not to care who followed him, maintaining a silent creeping pace if he were stalking something, and when he reached the clearing he began traversing it with his head down and his body bent almost double, moving steadily away from the river that had curved around to meet them and glided past, black and full of secrets, half a dozen yards away.

The landlord remained at the edge of the trees, shining his light in quick indecisive arcs, over first the water and then the clearing. Laurelie stood near him, following the hiker's progress as best she could. At one point when he abruptly crouched she nearly ran to him, but he only brushed the ground with his fingers and lifted them to his nose for a moment before continuing on again. He did this multiple times before reaching the far end of the clearing where the forest took up again. He disappeared then, and she simply counted breaths, hundreds of them before he reemerged again. He did not look up at her, was focused intently on the needled floor, but he shook his head in answer to her unspoken question and said, "He wasn't in there. No one was. He was here though. And there was a dog with him."

"A dog? What dog?" the landlord repeated.

The hiker ignored him, staggering not unlike a drunk as he followed an erratic path back across the clearing, dipping to touch the ground and smell his hand again and again. Reaching the river he skidded down its steep bank and then turned sharply left, following it back in the direction from which they'd come.

The trees rising up soon blocked him from view. Together Laurelie and the landlord scrambled down the slope after him and found him already yards ahead, hopscotching a tangle of exposed tree roots that reached down all along the bank to embrace the rocky waterline. The landlord's strong flashlight bathed their tops and deepened the shadows beneath, so that it looked like the ground had dropped away and the hiker was leaping through loops of thin black space.

And then suddenly the hiker was stopping, stooping,

reaching out his arms and leaning in. Whatever he sought there was obscured by a tree root that stuck out from the steep bank as wide and flat as the back of a chair.

Long seconds passed before he stood again, and this time there was something in his arms.

"Rowan!" the landlord called and then, leaping and tripping, he fell to his hands and knees. Rising again, he paced a single square foot of space impatiently, waiting for the hiker to pick his way back to them.

He was moving slowly now, his streaming eyes squeezed shut against the light the landlord kept trained on him. His nostrils were flared white and he was panting, but no one was looking at him. All eyes were fixed on the boy. He lay curled and still in the hiker's arms, and there was something small and dark curled in his own.

"Is he alright?" the landlord called.

"He's fine," the hiker said. "He's sleeping."

Still a yard from them, the hiker stopped. He raised his face as if they'd spoken, but his shaken gaze moved past them, tracking something in the clearing behind.

Laurelie turned around. She saw nothing, only blackness.

Then something growled. The sound seemed to come from everywhere at once, a guttural fury that did not end but rather slowly rose in pitch and intensified into a scream, before finally tailing off in a long sibilant hiss.

Far back in the clearing, two yellow eyes flared. Then they were gone, but only long enough to convey how fast the creature could move, reappearing again a moment later at the top of the bank.

The bobcat looked giant, standing there in the night with her teeth bared in fury and her eyes slitted against the light.

The landlord shouted. Splashing backward into the river, he raised his flashlight like a club. His light kaleidoscoped through the tops of the trees, illuminating not only his face but also the violence he intended.

Then the hiker was there, pushing the boy into his father's arms. There was anger in his face too, as in two long strides he climbed the bank. The bobcat did not move or even blink, but she made a noise as he came, a birdlike chirrup that he answered in the same voice before they slipped back into the darkness together.

The hiker led the way home, keeping yards ahead of them. The landlord came next, carrying his son, and Laurelie followed last, holding the flashlights and lighting the way for him. She kept peering over his shoulder at the animal in the boy's arms, finally deciding it was some sort of terrier, although in the dark and being so scrawny and filthy, it was hard to tell. Neither boy nor dog ever fully awoke, although periodically the animal would tremble, and then the boy's fingers would flex in its fur.

Back at the main house, the police checked the child over carefully. No broken bones, they said, and his pulse was steady, his skin wasn't hot or clammy and his pupils responded to light. Apart from a few scratches, they pronounced him healthy and said his stubborn sleep was a normal stress response, and the best medicine for him now. Still the tearful landlady wanted to make him wake and argued hotly for taking him to the emergency room. It took all of their combined efforts to convince her to wait until the morning.

The hiker stayed outside while they conferred, and once

they reached Laurelie's cottage he too fell asleep. Within minutes of pushing her windows wide and lying down on her bed he was out. But she was unable to follow him. Her mind wouldn't release the night, kept replaying scenes until finally she got up and released them, let them rise through her mind like bubbles and burst onto the page. She drew the black silk river with white wisps of a broken and bitten boy hovering over it. She drew the bobcat, barely visible, watching them from the trees. She drew the hushed oval of the clearing and the triangle of forest beyond, the giant tangle of brambles alive with the bob-kittens hidden at its heart. She drew the hiker lifting the boy from a cradle of roots, his strong brown arms shining like a god's in the half-light, and she drew his stricken expression when the bobcat appeared at the top of the bank, his anger when she screamed. She drew the landlord's flashlight raised like a club and his light whirling through the trees. And in her panels all that fury seemed indistinguishable from fear.

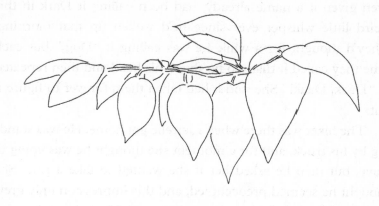

16

When she woke the next day the hiker wasn't there. Knowing he'd gone to check on the bobcat, she went up the hill to check on the boy. She found him crawling in the grass, barking in concert with the little dog he'd found the night before. In the light of day it wasn't black as she'd thought, but rather a very dark gray. The two of them were playing a game of fetch, although it wasn't clear most of the time who was fetching, or even who had the ball. The boy's mother hovered nearby sipping her coffee and watching them with anxious eyes. She told Laurelie she wasn't happy to be taking in a stray, that if the boy wanted a dog that much she could find him something far better, but he was already so attached to it and after his ordeal her husband was afraid of what he might do if they took it away. She said he'd even given it a name already, had been calling it Dark in this weird little whisper ever since he'd woken up that morning. They'd thought for a while he was calling it "Dog," but each time they called it that too he shook his head and then repeated it, "Daak, Daak!" She said it had taken them forever to figure it out.

The hiker was there when Laurelie got home. He was standing by his truck, and for a moment she thought he was going to leave, but then he asked her if she wanted to take a ride. She thought he seemed preoccupied, and this impression only grew once he'd turned north onto the river road. He drove so fast and with such a serious expression that she found herself imagining they were fleeing.

Then the road forked and he drove up a long slow gravel road to the top of a hill. There he stopped and they got out and sat on a grassy patch overlooking a granite outcropping that dripped like icing into the valley below. Wildflowers exploded down the slopes, looking more formidable than beautiful in their profusion and their autumn hues. His nostrils rippled tightly but his thoughts still seemed far away and so, seeking a path in, she asked him their names. Thistle, he told her, bee balm and goldenrod, tiger lily and dead nettle, staghorn sumac and switchgrass. Each word he spoke seemed to carry the prick of a hidden knife and looking at him she had an urge to squint and weave, as if seeing him through thick patterned glass.

On their way home they stopped at the organic farmer's market. He seemed to lighten as they perused tables and crates laden with speckled eggs and soft cheeses and loaves of bread still warm on the bottom and impossibly fat blueberries and ears of corn that smelled sweet enough to eat raw. But back at her cottage he cooked their meal like there was an ax at his neck, and then stayed on the porch long after they'd eaten, drinking mead and watching the sun go down.

She could not imagine what might be wrong, and each time she asked he only shrugged and said maybe nothing at all. He didn't seem to want company, and so she left him with his thoughts, did the dishes and then sat on the couch flipping through channels in the hopes of drawing him in. She found a nature program about Africa on PBS, and after a while he did come in and sat down on the floor beside her.

A group of lions stalked a herd of springbok across plains blanketed in sweet grasses. Half an hour later all the green was gone and the pools were shrinking and crocodiles hid in mud up to their eyeballs, watching their prey crowd in, made reckless by their need to drink. There were scenes of death then, while the blue sky dazzled and the salt pans deceived, looking full of water although they were bone dry. But some life survived, and then the rains returned and elephants filled the screen, kicking up puddles and lying their heavy bodies down.

When the credits rolled, she ran up to use the bathroom. She didn't hear him coming up the stairs, and so didn't know he was already there when she went into the dark bedroom and opened the windows.

She startled when he touched her. But his hands were hot, and slow, slipping down her arms, ruffling her skin like fine sandpaper, sliding through her sides to the valley of her belly, and when they glided up again and brushed her breasts, she had to open her mouth to breathe. The darkness fractured into a million sparks as his lips touched her neck. Her body felt heavy, like ripe fruit. And then he was lifting her, scattering kisses wherever his mouth could reach. They lay down on the bed, and blackness surrounded them, an infinite expanse, in which each touch was a miracle, of lips and hands and skin, and her eyes were wide, anticipating the moment their bodies created light.

Then there was great pressure. Her body went tight. He went still.

Only his thumbs moved, smoothing her temples.

Not broken. Wide open. No barriers at all.

Whether the words came from him or her own mind she wasn't sure, but when she looked across the darkness and found his determined eyes, she shuddered.

Then there was fire. It caught in their mouths and spilled over and spidered down, and when finally it subsided, his harsh breath still smoldered in her hair.

"We could leave," he murmured at some point later. "We could just—go."

"Go? Where?"

"I don't know. Anywhere. Africa, maybe."

"You mean . . . now?" She tried to imagine it.

He didn't say anything more. His breath stirred her hair like butterflies, alighting and lifting off again.

And after a while, they slept.

His sleep was restless all night, and finally at dawn he rose, and then she slept the kind of sleep nothing penetrated. Even after peeling herself from the sheets she sat on the bed for a long time, still saturated in dreams.

Going into the kitchen she found she could measure the

time that had amassed while she'd slept by the food arrayed there, all of it made from the leftovers of the night before. There was bruschetta with melted cheese and an omelet topped with corn salsa and a purple smoothie. But the cook himself wasn't there.

In a little while she saw him through the window coming up the trail, and her heart beat faster as she watched his long strides and remembered the night before. Then he stopped, and his head came up, and he turned and looked up the lane. She saw his nostrils flare, and for an instant his lips parted in what she imagined was a snarl. Then he bent his head so his hair covered his face and continued on again.

He did not come inside, however, but rather walked around to the tomato plants on the side of the house and crouched there. Coming out onto the porch, she heard him mouth-breathing. Before she could ask what was going on, the landlord's car came crawling along the lane, stray rocks popping beneath its tires like gunshots.

The car stopped before the cottage and the landlord got out. After nodding at Laurelie, he strolled over to the hiker. His hands were tucked in his trouser pockets and from them came a jingling sound.

He stood for a while, regarding the hiker with a small smile. "I still don't know how you did it," he finally said.

The hiker said nothing. Nor did he look up. Only his fingers moved, in and out of the tomato plants, pruning away the yellowed leaves.

Slowly the landlord's smile faded. Turning to face Laurelie, he said, "Violet and I don't want you taking Rowan into those woods anymore. You should know it's no place for a little boy. I'll call Montague's building and grounds guys in the morning, see if they'll come out and trap that—that *animal.*" He shuddered as he said these last words, causing another faint jingle.

His eyes were round and protruding, his neck thrust forward as he spoke, and Laurelie was still struggling to absorb these signs of his conviction, so at odds with what she herself knew to be true, when from behind him, the hiker stood.

"Leave her alone," he said, and his voice was a growl. "She won't hurt the boy. Or anyone."

The landlord swiveled in surprise. Then his eyes gathered light as understanding crept in. "Your intentions were good, son," he said. "But frankly, you should have known better as well. Approaching a wild animal like that! You could have been mauled. A bite from that thing—" He shuddered again, setting off another jingle.

The hiker's nostrils flared white, and as they watched his eyes gathered tears. "She'd never do that," he said, rapidly blinking them back.

"It's probably sick, in fact," the landlord went on, "to have attacked us like that. It probably has rabies, or—or—or mange, or something like that."

"She didn't attack us!" The hiker shook his head hard and now a few tears spilled over, tracking down his cheeks and spattering the ground. He didn't bother to wipe them, didn't even seem to notice them, his words tripping over themselves as he said, "She was only trying to warn me about an intruder, that's all. She doesn't know you. She wouldn't ever hurt you or any human though," he went on as the landlord's eyes widened. "You have to believe me."

He sounded desperate and looked it too, with his eyes streaming and his nostrils flaring as if he smelled something terrible, his mouth twisting as if he tasted it too.

Suddenly, Laurelie felt afraid.

But the landlord only looked confused. He turned to her and widened his eyes and shook his head, as if to ask her what she thought they should do about this situation.

When she looked away, he said, "Well." And then nodded a little. Looked down at his shoes and rocked on his heels and said, "Well, I'll take that into consideration, son, I certainly will."

He looked toward his car then and shifted his weight as if in anticipation of his first step, only to freeze as the hiker came hurtling toward him over the tomato plants. The landlord's hands came up but the hiker came no closer. He never even slowed. He ran down the lane another fifty yards before he stopped and turned back.

"Whisper something!" he called.

When the landlord only frowned, the hiker repeated it.

"Why exactly am I supposed to whisper?" the landlord asked Laurelie.

Down the lane the hiker called, "You said, 'Why exactly am I supposed to whisper?' Except you didn't. Do it again, as quietly as you can."

The landlord's eyebrows rose. After a moment, he stepped close to the porch stairs, at the top of which stood Laurelie. This time he turned his back to the hiker, and whispered a date so quietly that even Laurelie wasn't sure she heard it correctly.

But the hiker's voice rang out loud and clear. "December 21, 1933."

"My father's birthday," the landlord said, turning back around. "So what's the trick?" he called.

"There's no trick," the hiker replied. "I hear better than you, that's all."

He began walking back to them. "All my senses are better,"

he said, "That's how I found your son. And that's how I know the bobcat won't hurt him, or anyone. I can see it and hear it and smell it and taste it and feel it too."

The landlord watched him come, his expression shifting like lava through surprise and disbelief and dismay. And although she'd already come to know it, Laurelie felt a little of those same emotions as well, because it was one thing to have privately believed something and another to finally hear it voiced publicly.

From the silence, other sounds emerged. The hiker's soft steps along the dirt lane, the skitter of a chipmunk in an oak tree, the slow buzz of a bumblebee. The distant barks of a dog and a boy up on the main house lawn. The sunlight was full of color, the breeze light and voluminous, and in that moment all of Laurelie's own senses seemed to be heightened as well.

"Have you seen a doctor about this?" the landlord asked.

He'd seen many, the hiker told him. He'd been sick for a long time. The doctors had determined it was caused by a virus, but that was all they'd figured out. They'd said he would either die or recover, and eventually he'd recovered. But his senses never had.

He'd reached them by then, and was standing very still, looking at the landlord with his shoulders high and his hands fisted at his sides. His eyes were wet and his nostrils were flickering and his mouth was open, tasting him. It was a reaction that by now Laurelie had come to perceive as normal, and yet with its cause laid bare and the landlord there and aware of it, its effect was newly disconcerting. And the fact that the hiker must know she felt this only made it even worse.

The landlord took a step back.

The hiker closed the gap. "Now that you understand, what

are you going to do?" he said, and Laurelie could almost see him bristling, hissing.

"About the—the bobcat?" The landlord could not look for long at the hiker's face, and so his gaze bounced around from there to the trail to the car behind him, as if looking for somewhere safe. "Well, I definitely appreciate your, ah, special insights. The animal's no danger, you say? I suppose there's no need for us to be hasty, then."

The hiker said nothing, watching him, his nostrils pulsing angrily.

"I should be going," the landlord said. "Violet's expecting me."

Laurelie sank down on the porch stair and watched the landlord's car crawl back up the lane. Above the main house the sun had reached its zenith and hung there like a ball of fire. She lay back and closed her eyes, welcoming its heat, feeling it anesthetize her brain and melt her knotted muscles into the warm porch boards. For a while that was all she felt, and then there was something else, a current of cold threading through the warmth, a sound so thin and high and keening it almost seemed she imagined it.

"Hawk," the hiker murmured, and she opened her eyes to see it gliding low over the hill. And then, so fast it had already happened by the time it occurred, the bird dropped to the grass and was soaring away again with a tiny body twisting in its talons.

"Mole."

It must have been in the dirt, the hiker told her. The sun was lowering and the cold was growing and he was sitting beside her on the porch stair with his long limbs tightly folded, telling her things she'd so long wanted to know, and that somehow now no longer seemed to matter at all. How some rich man had bought a tiny island in northern Maine and paid the hiker's family to build a living greenhouse on it, because he wanted to grow tropical plants surrounded by snow. How it had been a big job and that's why they'd taken it, even though it had come so late in the season that they'd had to rush to finish it before first frost. It had been the summer after the hiker's freshman year at college and he'd been getting ready to go back. They'd spent two weeks on that island, from dawn until dark, his dad working the backhoe, digging out a six-foot house-sized hole, and then the hiker running the heating cables through it that would keep the soil a constant sixty degrees. It had rained the whole time; he'd been covered in mud. It had gotten in his water, his food. And somewhere in all that dirt, he said, there must have been a virus, ancient and long ago buried inside some other ancient life's remains. Because three days later, the same morning he was supposed to leave for school, he'd gotten sick. The fever had struck so hard and quickly that he'd had a seizure right there on the kitchen floor. His dad had held him while his mom called 911. The hospital had gotten the fever down, but even afterward his body had still felt like it was burning. They'd done some tests and then sent him home, saying it would probably go away. But instead every few days he'd get another fever, the fire spreading over his skin until it consumed him. He always knew when one was coming on because of the triggers. One time a UPS guy had come to the door and the hiker smelled his aftershave all the way upstairs, in his room on the second floor. Another time, lying on his bed, he'd watched a tiny spider on the ceiling lift its leg and tap the thread of its web, and heard the whole thing hum.

Based on his blood work the doctors knew it was a virus, but it was one they'd never seen before. And so there was no medicine, no cure. Over time the fevers had grown weaker and less frequent, but the burning never stopped. And without the fevers, the doctors could find nothing wrong. They said there was some lingering swelling, that's all. They suggested neurological testing. The hiker swallowed hard then, the motion traveling down his body as he told her they claimed hallucinations sometimes resulted from extended illness, and prescribed antipsychotic medication for him.

He stopped going to doctors then. For a long time he'd stayed at home. He'd moved into the downstairs room, and never left it. The input, he told her, was just too overwhelming. Everything stank, or deafened, or blinded him, everything he touched pierced him like a knife, and even plain water tasted like poison. By then it was spring, and one day his mother came in and opened his window. Just to see, she'd said.

Amazingly, it had helped. The input was if anything more intense, but somehow it made more sense to him. He began spending time outside, first hours and then entire days, drawn to the woods where there were no humans to see him as sick, their reactions only making him feel sicker. He began sleeping out there with his dog, began staying for weeks at a time. Alone in the woods, his fear and panic diminished, and finally the burning began to differentiate, so that he could distinguish the individual strands of information coming in. He began to understand how his senses had changed, and what they could now do.

He learned to survive in the wild, to eat only what vegetation his senses told him was okay, and to track and hunt down animal prey.

He got a lot better then, he said. His senses still flared at every stimulus, but now he could assimilate them, and instead of panicking could determine which and how much he could bear. He began returning home for short periods, and then for longer ones. His parents were so relieved they rebuilt their downstairs all in unprocessed woods and glass and clays, using only materials that didn't smell abhorrent to him. They were already organic gardeners, but now he'd bring home meat for them to eat, deer and rabbit and small birds. Eventually he even started working in their landscaping business again.

But the human smells were just too complex, he said. Everything people did stank of corruption. That's why, after a while, he always had to go back to the woods again.

He turned then and gazed down at her.

And so, she thought, looking back at him, what has changed? In the telling his story had felt so physical, raging over them like a force of nature. But now that it had receded again, nothing had changed. Only the light. Everything looked deeper, sadder and richer too, everything coated in the residue of his remembered pain. How clearly one saw a world in its twilight.

Whatever he sought in her eyes, he must have found, for he lay back against the stairs beside her. His nose pulsed softly, nearly infinitesimally. He closed his eyes, and she did the same.

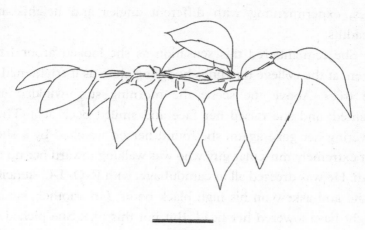

17

Laurelie released a long pent-up breath as she walked down the path from the Montague administration offices. It seemed as if she'd been holding it forever, and now she took great gulps of air. She'd just officially graduated from college, having handed in her honors thesis, a compendium of panels she'd been up until dawn putting the final touches on. Then she'd fallen asleep and dreamed of flying. Not flying exactly, bouncing really, first an epiphany of realizing she could spring with her legs and soar into the air and then the crystalline uncertainty of descent, so much faster than rising and with death at the end, until she discovered that falling was in fact simply high-speed floating and she was strong enough to land, after which she began leaping, arcing off the sides of buildings and riffling through the tops of trees, experimenting with different angles and heights and breadths.

She remembered this sensation as she looked around the green, at the college buildings huddling close as if frightened of the trees. Above the scene the morning sun twinkled and beamed, and she raised her face and smiled back at it. Then, lowering her gaze again, she found herself watched by a short but extremely muscular guy who was walking toward her up the path. He was dressed all in camouflage, with R-O-T-C stenciled white and askew on his high black boots. On another day she might have lowered her head. But not this one. She picked up her pace, but not in fear; she was thinking of the hiker. He'd be returning soon. He'd arrived at her cottage just as she was leaving and was at that moment cajoling the bobcat and her kittens into the large wooden crate he'd constructed for them. By tonight they would all be safe in his woods, settling into their new home. Laurelie herself would have an entire month to live there with them before graduate school started and she had to return to Montague.

When her cell phone chirruped she fumbled for it in her backpack, imagining for an instant he was calling because he'd felt her thinking of him. That it wasn't him but rather her landlord hardly deflated her at all. Nor did the man's asking her to stop by his office before she left campus in order to sign her lease for the coming year. The task would not take long; the ivy-covered building in which he worked was only a few paces away.

His secretary said he was expecting her. Walking down the quiet hall she heard his voice and found the door was partway open. Knocking softly, she pushed it wider. Her landlord was sitting behind an ornate desk on the other side of the room. When he caught sight of her, he bid her enter and smiled.

She imagined herself shrinking as she crossed the floor. Her feet sank deep into the enormous blue carpet, its creamy border twined with golden vines and at its center a coiled and snarling dragon. But also the room, being so large and nearly a perfect cube, seemed to alter the proportions of the things inside it. Despite the bright day, it was dim as well, the only light a matrix of small windows on the far wall that glowed but did not penetrate, and on the desk a small lamp shining green. There was a fireplace in one corner but it was cold now, and the armchairs before it were full of shadows. She imagined as she passed them she heard the murmurs of prior administrators still lingering.

Not until she'd reached the desk did she realize a small gray-haired man was sitting in one of them.

She stepped back in surprise as he rose to greet her.

"Laurelie," said the landlord, "I'd like you to meet Dr. Waters. We were college roommates years ago. Back in the dark ages."

Both men laughed.

"Dr. Waters was in the area this morning," the landlord went on, "so I asked him to drop by. We've had a nice talk, and now he'd like to talk with you." He clasped his hands in the small circle of light on his desk, continuing, "Dr. Waters is a virologist, Laurelie. He works at the CDC. He's done some truly groundbreaking research there over the past twenty years. Twice he's even been short-listed for the Nobel Prize."

"Thank you, Owen," the doctor said. "It's nice to meet you, Laurelie. Owen is right. I'd very much like to talk to you. And to your friend too."

Slowly, then, the relative proportions of the room and its contents inverted. The walls receded and the living bodies loomed, while the whispers of the dead ones swelled until a sound like static filled the room.

"CDC?" Her own voice came out cracked and bleak. "That's—that's Center for Disease Control."

"Actually it's Centers with an 's,'" the doctor said with a smile. "We're a multi-site organization."

"Laurelie, wait a minute!" the landlord called. She paid him no mind, passing over the dragon's back and crossing the twining golden vines. Then her hand closed around the door handle, and she was grateful for its cold hard smoothness as she swung the door wide.

Halfway through the doorway she heard the doctor remark, "Of course, with any virus there is a public safety issue at stake. But of primary concern to you, I'm sure, would be how great a risk there still is to your friend."

She stopped.

"Yes. Now you see why I'd like to talk to you."

Slowly she turned around, her mind flashing cinematics of outbreaks and quarantines in hazy staccato red.

"I'd suggest we keep the door closed," the virologist murmured, "for privacy."

After a moment she did as he suggested, but remained there, standing with her back against it.

"Are you sure you won't sit down?" the doctor said.

She shook her head.

"Well then, let me start with a disclaimer. Until I examine your friend I can't make a specific diagnosis. However, based on the limited history Owen provided, I can make some general predictions. Owen said your friend was previously diagnosed with a virus of unknown origin. He thought this probably occurred a few years ago now?"

The doctor's gaze met hers. When she didn't respond, it attached itself high on the wall above her head. "Owen also said your friend appears to have lingering symptoms, specifically one or more senses functioning beyond normal human range."

He began to pace now, back and forth over the dragon's back. His body was slight as a greyhound's, its motions small but brisk. "The question we must therefore ask ourselves is what this schedule of onset and symptoms suggests.

"We have at our disposal over two hundred years of viral research. And what have we learned from it? First, that the virus is the oldest and most abundant biological entity on Earth. There are millions currently in existence, although we've studied only a tiny fraction in any detail." He was warming to his discourse, picking up speed, his hands gesturing in rapid punctuation of his speech.

"Second, we know the virus is a highly specialized organism. Most can target only a single cell type within a single species, which statistically, of course, will be non-human. However, viruses can evolve, and thus so can their targets. Rabies, avian flu, and smallpox are all examples of viruses that have evolved to target multiple species, including humans.

"Third, although we think of a virus as a living organism, in fact it only partially fulfills the requirements for life. It contains genetic material, the medium by which instructions are transmitted from one generation of organisms to the next, but it lacks the internal cellular structure necessary to reproduce on its own. To do so it must borrow the machinery of other organisms. And this of course is done through the process of infection."

Here the landlord cleared his throat, but the virologist paid him no attention. "Regardless of the type of cell it infects," he went on, "each virus particle has only one single purpose, and it is one it achieves alone. For there is no communication at all between virus particles. Each acts wholly in isolation, seeking a host cell to penetrate and then copy itself inside, using the cell's internal machinery. Typically replication continues until the cell's resources have been depleted. The viral copies that have been produced then each go out and seek their own host cell, either within the same host or a new one. This ability to be transferred between hosts is what makes a virus contagious."

Again the landlord cleared his throat, and for an instant Laurelie wanted to throttle him.

"However, we must also keep in mind," the virologist said, "that the infected host doesn't usually die as a result of contagion. Mortality depends on a number of factors, including the speed and profusion with which the virus replicates, the cell type it targets, and the immune system's defense. Rabies, for example, kills because it bursts the walls of the brain cells in which it replicates. Influenza, on the other hand, typically does not kill even though it replicates more profusely, because it does so in cells of the respiratory system. Ebola, on the other hand, kills so overwhelmingly not because of its own actions but because of those of the host's own immune system, which responds with such a massive release of cytokines that the integrity of the infected vascular cells is compromised—basically causing its own body to bleed to death."

The doctor smiled into the landlord's shocked expression and went on. "Contrary to the impression lent by such extreme examples, however, most viruses only cause death when there are weak immune systems at play, such as in the very young, or elderly, or sick. Healthy immune systems will typically recover completely. This of course is in the interest of both species' survival, in the virus's case because it increases the amount of reproduction that occurs, and also the likelihood of transference to new hosts. Usually a healthy immune system will eradicate the infection within a few weeks, but during this time many instances of transfer will take place. Viruses can enter our bodies through the mouth, nose, eyes, or urogenital openings, or through bites or wounds that breach the skin. They can come, or course, from direct contact with an infected body, but also indirectly from all the environments where its infected fluids and microbes may have been shed."

Waters stopped pacing abruptly. His eyes were the brightest things in the room. "Now. Given this basic background, let us consider the particular case of your friend. He appeared to have largely recovered from his initial viral infection, but his lingering symptoms indicate there were complications. These may be reflective of a secondary condition, which can sometimes result from the process of viral elimination by the host body—collateral damage, if you will. For example, infection by the influenza virus will in rare cases result in Guillain-Barre syndrome, a paralytic condition resulting from the immune system's own reaction, which damages the peripheral nervous system. I must emphasize here," the doctor added, looking straight at Laurelie, "that such post-viral diseases are usually life-threatening, and thus the earlier they're diagnosed, the better."

Now the virologist dropped his gaze to the floor. Frowning, he said, "This scenario is unlikely in your friend's case, however. For although it would explain his continuing symptoms, such secondary conditions are rare in healthy young individuals. This fact makes a chronic or latent infection more likely. Chronic infections, such as Hepatitis C and HIV, are ones that even a strong immune system can't fully eradicate, either because the viral replication process suppresses or evades the host's immune system, or because it yields too many mutations for the host's system to fight. While these continuous infections may not kill the host, they do drain its internal defenses and are associated with long-term damage or disease, including cancer.

"Far more interesting from my point of view, however," the doctor went on, resuming his pacing, "is the very rarest instance of chronic infection, that is, the latent one." He smiled. "These viruses are the Einsteins of their kind, for they have learned to hide. The body cannot fight them unless they are active, and they've developed the ability to fall dormant for indefinite periods of time. We know the least about these viruses simply because they are the most rare. Herpes is probably the best-known example. It is an ancient virus that has been infecting humans since long before we could even call ourselves human. Like rabies, it infects neurons, but unlike rabies there is no deadly outcome, because long ago it learned both to evade the immune system and to avoid great collateral damage. In fact the herpes virus has adapted so well that more than thirty percent of the population carries it today."

The deep affection in the doctor's voice made sharp contrast with the information it conveyed. "Of course, in order to survive, even latent viruses must eventually replicate and transfer, and to do so activation must occur. We believe activation of latent viruses is triggered by external stimuli, such as sunlight or stress. At that point the body will present symptoms and briefly become contagious, before the virus falls dormant again."

Now he turned and appraised Laurelie. He was quiet for some moments, holding her in his gaze. When he spoke again his voice was dry and clinical. "Unfortunately, as I said earlier, without a detailed examination, I can't determine what type of virus your friend had, or may still have. I can, however, with a few drops of your own blood, determine whether you've already been infected."

At his words this same fluid attempted to flee, rushing back to her heart from her limbs and brain. "But my senses are normal," she said dizzily.

The virologist chuckled. "Yes, well, oddly enough, some viruses are remarkably difficult to catch. Still, you should be aware that there is a definite possibility of transmission eventually occurring, if it hasn't already. Human fluids are very highly effective vectors." His eyes grew brighter now. "And some viruses will go dormant for an interval following infection, an adaptation that helps increase transference, but also means that it may take some time for you to display symptoms. You've known your friend only a few months, I believe? In any event, if it is already hiding somewhere inside you, the best tests we've developed will detect its faint markers in your blood."

"No." She was shaking her head. "His virus didn't work like that. He got sick from it right away."

"How could he possibly know that?" the virologist shot back.

"Because he got it from the dirt, on this old island where—"

She closed her mouth with a snap, realizing too late how she'd been baited.

"An interesting hypothesis." The doctor smiled. "We can take samples from this island as well."

Across the varnished darkness of the office, the windows glowed like tiny dying suns. Laurelie imagined they'd once borne a light so hot and bright it had been impossible for life to survive it. She imagined the hiker's cabin in the cool dark woods, with its small patch of garden in which the bob-kittens would play.

"What about his children?" she said softly. "Will they have it too?"

"Ah." The doctor fairly purred, pure pleasure in his voice. "You've hit upon our philosopher's stone. We've known for a long time that a few rare viruses can hide inside genes and thus alter the genetic makeup of individuals. But only recently have we found evidence that some can hide inside our chromosomes and so be passed into our progeny, potentially impacting genetics on a far larger scale than we ever believed possible."

He glanced back and forth between Laurelie and the landlord, a faint smile playing across his lips. "Can you imagine," he said, "a sense-enhancing virus persistent enough to alter the evolution of our entire human species?"

She stood on the steps of the administration building, feeling the late summer sun bake the skin of her shoulders even as the fall air sprouted goose bumps on her limbs. Just as the weather couldn't commit to a single season, so was she now trapped in a modality in which nothing was known for certain, only possible or likely or believed. Frozen by indecision, only her eyes moved, traveling the route her feet would take down the gravel path and across the green to her bike. Which she'd then mount and somehow coerce into motion—

And then?

She was already over an hour late getting home. Checking her cell phone, she saw a missed call from the hiker. She thought of the bobcat, frightened, pacing in her crate, and finally forced her feet to move. But halfway across the green, she sank down onto a wooden bench again and pressed her fingers hard to the fresh hole in her arm. The sting from the blood the doctor had drawn focused her mind, and she imagined for a moment actually doing it—keeping the secret. For a day, a week, a month, maybe even years, as long as it took before the moment came when she grew feverish and her entire body became hypera-ware. So that she no longer needed to tell him at all, because he'd already sense it. And she'd sense that he sensed it, and he'd sense that she sensed him sensing it. In her mind the perfect communion they could achieve spiraled down in recursing sequence, like an infinite strand of DNA.

But the image shattered. For how could she keep a secret that might be life-threatening to him? Still, each time his cell phone rang she shuddered. Six times she nearly hung up before he answered, and when finally he did, and his voice slid deep inside her ear, her lips trembled and her heart clattered and tears started hot in her eyes.

"Hi," she said, "hi," lifting her feet onto the bench and hugging her knees, wishing she could squeeze herself small enough to slip through the holes in the mouthpiece and pop out on the other side.

"Where are you?" he said, and she heard a rustle and a thud, as if he'd jumped down from something.

"Still at school."

He sounded so incredibly clear. Her own thoughts were so tangled, such an ugly snarl without order or coherency. She tried to find the starting thread. "I'm—I'm calling about my landlord," she finally said.

"I've been thinking about that too," he said.

"No, it's worse! I mean—" she said, leaning forward so far she almost tumbled off the bench, "he called me into his office. Just now. That's where I've been. There was a doctor there, a Dr. Waters, a scientist, a virologist, from the CDC."

Laurelie stopped then. But the hiker said nothing. There

was only his breathing. And so she took a deep breath of her own and went on.

"He wants to talk to you. He—he—he took my blood. He says you might still be sick. Infected. He says you could still have the virus inside you, or even if you don't, you could get cancer from it, or be paralyzed, or—or worse."

Now there was no sound from the phone at all. There was only silence, and it roared, echoing and colliding with all the thoughts and emotions she imagined he was having.

But when finally he did speak, he only sounded sad. "He thinks I might still be contagious? After all this time?"

"He said it's a possibility. He wants you to come in as soon as possible for tests."

"I could infect you—"

She shook her head, shook away that terrible sadness welling beneath his words. "Nothing's certain yet. Not until you get tested."

It seemed forever before he spoke again, and when he did his voice was so quiet she couldn't hear anything in it but the words.

"If I get tested, they'll never leave me alone. I'll be their lab rat."

"But they can help you, if you're sick." She wouldn't even speak the other possibility.

And then, horribly, she pictured it. The hiker trapped in a hospital ward with his body slowly wasting away, and not even from his virus but rather the suffocation, the asphyxiation, of being surrounded by so much pain.

"Never mind then," she whispered. "Let's just forget it."

"It's too late," she heard him say, as if from a great distance.

"We'll go away. We'll disappear. We can go anywhere. We can go to Africa, like you wanted." For a moment she could see the rich red African dirt, feel it beneath her feet.

"It's not safe. Not for you. I have to go now, and you can't come with me."

"But I have to!" she burst out, feeling everything important to her swell and distort until all of it was grotesque.

"That's not true," he said. "You have to stay."

How could he know that? He couldn't see or smell or touch her. Had he been within reach she would have struck him for his certainty. Instead it was her own body that crumbled as she listened to the last words he spoke, that drifted to the bench in soft little piles of dust and ashes as the last echoes of his voice faded away.

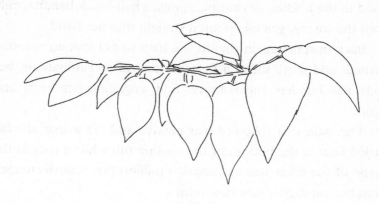

18

For a time, there was only dark and light.

Dark.

Light.

Dark.

Light.

And then her phone rang. "Hello, Laurelie. This is Dr. Water's secretary. He asked me to tell you that your tests came back negative. And that he would still like very much to talk with your friend. Thank you, and have a nice day!"

It was a hellish awakening, not hearing the hiker's voice. She tried not to listen, but understanding crept in. She got out of bed then. Weak as an old woman, she tottered downstairs and stood in the kitchen devouring things, a half-black banana, milk from the carton, granola poured straight into her hand.

Back upstairs again she drew a bath so hot that any motion burned, and there sat in a fiery concert of recriminations, her body still but her anger active, fully engaging her heart and mind.

The pain that followed was passive and far worse; she lay curled fetal at the bottom of the cooling tub while a root in the shape of the hiker was extracted, a million tiny tendrils tugged from her capillaries, arteries, veins.

But afterward, once she rose chilled and shivering from the bath and tentatively flexed those conduits, she felt no weakness, no lingering pain. On the contrary she felt cauterized, cavernous. Thoughts whistled softly through her carved-out spaces and rivulets of emotion trickled down them, tinkling like chimes.

Sometimes as those first days passed, she'd suddenly picture him, in one of the spaces he'd so often been. In her kitchen, her living room, getting out of his truck in her yard, walking toward her up the trail. She'd smell the forest scent of his skin and hear his fast mouth breaths. And then it would be back to the scalding bath again.

Sometimes, as days turned to weeks, she'd imagine calling him. Savoring the delicious shock of it, the sudden rush and thrum of ardor at hearing him say her name. Except always there followed the sinking surety that he wouldn't answer the phone. That he was gone, lost to her. Lost to the world. For all practical purposes he existed now only in her imagination, and there was some small comfort to be had in the fact that there at least he would remain, immutable, preserved forever in the black soil of her mind.

Then, as weeks turned to months, there came times when it was enough to know he was safe, hidden away with his dog and bobcat in his cabin in the woods. And that for as long as he lived he would always be safe, because no one could find him there, not without her. No one even knew his name.

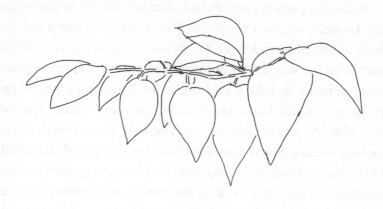

19

Then, of course, came graduate school. From the start it looked a lot like college, albeit the surfaces were a little slicker, a little shinier. It felt like a stage and all the actors looked like amateurs, trying too hard at the parts they played. But after a while it began to feel, in a strange way, real, and she began to notice how much had changed. Unlike college, there was no longer the anonymity of a lecture hall; now the same dozen students surrounded her every day, and all of them sought to stand out in some way. In college the professors had been distant bodies, some godlike and others alien, but now they were indolent alphas lying close among the pack, and their only significant motion some days was a cuff to end the worst infighting.

Following patterns established after her assault, in the beginning Laurelie sought exit routes. But it was as if she'd lost the talent for it. She no longer knew how to flourish completely apart from the world. Her dreams were porous and her solitude was even more so. Like a cat burglar the hiker crept into all her private spaces, his body, his motions, his most minute interactions with the world, and the joy she took from reincarnating him was intense. She'd draw him back into the world, hundreds of fast charcoal sketches, imagining him in every possible reconfiguration, as a tracker locating the lost, a chef creating innovative meals, a doctor discovering impossible cures, a spy protecting his country from terrorists, a detective with an infallible eye for guilt and innocence. But although these sessions were cathartic, the returning tide of loss was always stronger than the release had been. And slowly then it came to pass that the more of him she tried to evoke, the less actually emerged. She had rubbed her memories of him so raw that they began to twist and fray, and she imagined they were actually turning against her, seeking to strangle whatever life remained in her like some bitter, dying vine.

After that it became necessary to resist him. And so each time he came to mind she'd put down her work and stroke her cats until they were sprawled on their backs with their chins outstretched and cricket chirps sounding in their purrs. Or she'd go up the hill and play with Rowan and Dark. She no longer babysat the boy because he'd started preschool and her stipend now paid her rent, but his mother was always happy for her to take him for free. They'd go outside bundled in layers of cotton and fleece and play fetch on the hill, stripping down to their T-shirts for the rare jewel hours when the sun gained its height, hours that became less and less until eventually it hardly crept above the trees at all. But although both boy and dog would beg her, she never took them down to the river, and not only because she'd promised. She never went herself either; it was hard enough just passing by the trail each day and willing away the image that came unbidden of Ophelia floating down cold black water.

Idle hands, she reminded herself often. But nature was never idle. And as autumn progressed it grew into a red carpet affair. Colors she'd never noticed before shimmied in the valleys and dazzled up and down the broad sides of mountains. She'd stay outside drawing all day, fashioning her deciduous trees like fairy queens and giving them glamorous names like Salomie and Amaranth, Sunglow and Chartreuse, while her tall austere ever-greens bent down to stare, whispering in awe. She drew the wallflowers too, all those plain green bushes of summer that had burst into the limelight now, their leaves lit up like bonfires in the yards all over town.

By November everything was dead, everything some shade of brown. The mornings dawned frigid and frost lingered in the shadows all day. But roots still beat like hearts beneath the ground, and so she drew gold in the brown, and silver in the green, and stayed out each day until the encroaching darkness forced her inside.

Now there were many waking hours spent in overheated rooms, and she could no longer avoid an awareness of what was going on inside of them. She even developed a favorite class, a seminar on graphic novels. The other students in it often had interesting things to say, referencing Spiegelman and Otomo, Warhol and Lichtenstein; even Whedon and Watterson had been raised. The professor let them all have play. She permitted no biases, said it didn't matter if someone was alive or dead, canonized or disregarded, all that mattered was what *you* said. And as time went by Laurelie found she had things she wanted to add to the conversation. Sometimes the perfect remark would form in her brain and her body would still be throbbing with it long after the topic had moved on. As if sensing her inner turmoil, the professor sometimes asked her to speak, and displays of idiocy on these occasions brought the entire pack baying joyfully. The first time it happened Laurelie had produced a half-coherent response while experiencing the embarrassment of her body as if it were happening to someone else, and then spent the rest of the day formulating what she should have said instead. After that she followed the discussion closely and always maintained a careful argument in her head, so that when she was called upon at least her remarks emerged well-manicured, and while they weren't often taken up for further debate, they were never again openly ridiculed.

Never, that was, until one Friday shortly after Thanksgiving when she was accosted after class by a short guy in thick black glasses. His name was Scottie and he was a Londoner and she regarded him approaching with some trepidation, not only because he was shaking his head but also because his opinions were usually caustic enough that the rest of the pack gave him a wide berth.

They'd been discussing omniscience, that all-knowing point of view from which so many traditional stories were told, and just before she let them go Professor Prince had asked Laurelie if she had anything to add. Laurelie had said only that she found it a particularly difficult point of view, because the space of all-knowingness was infinite while that of the page was so limited. She'd thought it was a rather obvious thing to say, but apparently Scottie thought otherwise. Stopping in front of her desk, he said loudly, "Frankly Laurelie, I don't see how the size of the page is relevant at all."

If he hadn't stuffed his hands in his pockets, she probably would have ignored him. But something about the way he did it made it seem like he didn't mean to be belligerent, that he honestly did want to know.

So she told him she had simply meant that when you left things out, all the negative space of what you didn't choose to show was as meaningful to the viewer as what you did show. And so it seemed impossible for what was on the page to represent omniscience without it coming across as ignorant or biased and offending some people—

Scottie howled then, literally threw back his head and extended the long vowel of his negation. The last student in the room jumped liked he'd been goosed and scurried out the door.

"Art," Scottie said urgently, "isn't about perfection. It only has to be interesting. Mm," he nodded, apparently liking the sound of this, "and anyway isn't the space of any point of view infinite? Take mine, for example. You have no idea what I'll do next."

He grinned then, and his expression was so mischievous that Laurelie couldn't help but smile back. "Sure," she said, "but most of it wouldn't be art."

Now he laughed, and bouncing on the balls of his feet, told her he knew a guy in the film department whom he thought she might like. He was going to meet him for a drink in a few minutes, he said, and she should come along if she liked.

She could feel herself trembling as they entered the pub, and found she couldn't look directly at the bar, but rather had to confront it through mirror behind it, half-fearing and half-hoping to see the hiker's body coiled somewhere.

But the stools were all bare, and so were the tables, including the one against the back wall behind the little stage where the door onto the alley opened. Neither was the little pub dim and crowded, as it had been the last time she was there. On this chilly late November day it was bright with afternoon light and completely deserted. There wasn't even a waitress at that hour, Scottie told her as they crossed the floor; they had to go and order their drinks at the bar. They headed then for a booth against the windows where a tall, bearded man sat alone. Soft rock was being piped through speakers mounted in the corners of the room, and Scottie was humming along and gripping the straps of his shoulder bag so tightly that she suspected with surprise he was nervous too.

Two drinks later she thought she understood. Scottie had feelings for Will. And while Will himself was largely inscrutable, she suspected those feelings were reciprocated. Will was in AA, and so none of them were drinking alcohol, but rather mugs of hot cider, which were fragrant and soothing. Sitting there, two hours flew by, full of an animated conversation in which they all shared their opinions about the responsibility of contemporary art, but threaded through as well with a second conversation, a cautious and unspoken one going on between the two men, and to which she was only a spectator.

The following Friday afternoon Scottie invited her to come to the pub with them again. This time another grad student joined them as well, a friend of Will's from the philosophy department, with whom she suspected them, as the afternoon progressed, of trying to set her up. But if they were, it was such a lighthearted attempt that she didn't really mind, and neither did they seem to when she ignored it.

The next week another grad student showed up, and more came in the weeks after that. By January they were pushing tables together and calling it their Friday faculty meetings—only half-joking since all of them were shouldering significant teaching responsibilities so that their advisors could spend their time less tediously engaged. Settling in, they would complain of the piles of tests and papers they had to grade, and the undergrads who, despite the great show the professor put on in class, soon figured out the difference between taskmaster and decision maker, and then came to them arguing for better grades. Laurelie and Scottie would cast each other guilty looks, for their complaints seemed weaker by comparison, their labor consisting largely of monitoring studio classes and helping the students with their art one on one. Indeed Laurelie mostly enjoyed it; each student was like a puzzle, finding the right artists to show, the right words to deconstruct their art and make it open up, so the student would see it working just like his or her own.

The conversations didn't linger long on onerous topics, but seemed to touch on everything else, lasting late into the night until the little pub was bursting and the bartender was shouting, "Last call!"

Left to her own devices, Laurelie would have shied away from belonging to this or any group, and perhaps Scottie understood this, for he always came to fetch her at the end of class on Fridays. And always afterward, she was glad to have gone, for the intellectual connections forged there were always so cerebral and intense. Probably there were corporal connections being forged as well, but for Laurelie this was purely a gathering of minds seeking to discharge the subjectivity they'd been accumulating all week. Their areas of expertise spanned so many fields of humanities and science, and visually it was a motley crew as well, some people armored in collars and ties while others swaggered around in leather. And they spoke such different technical languages; probably the most interesting part was watching them try to make themselves understood. In the process a subject would be stripped and redressed again in a way that bore little resemblance to the original, so that even topics upon which she couldn't dwell alone, like love or sex or sickness or death, yielded no painful effects. She imagined those meetings as outside the realm of reality, as if they weren't really humans assembled there but rather their ideal projections outside themselves, observing their bodies' own natural patterns and rhythms.

In real life, however, she was still subject to random possessions. There was no predicting it; she might be drawing or doing some small task about the cottage or kicking her way through piles of snow with Rowan and Dark, when for the space of a heartbeat it was *his* limbs she moved, *his* thoughts forming in her head, *his* eyes through which she suddenly saw the world. And yet as painful as this experience was, as soon it was over she'd long for it back, struggle to return to it as if to a dream and then, still full of the suffering that follows failure, grow desperate with a need to finally exorcise him.

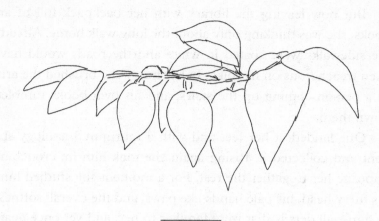

20

A handful of dry brown leaves skittered at the bottom of the library stairs, hunched there against the wind. Snow had just started to fall, hours earlier than predicted, a curtain of crystals as tiny as pinheads and so dense it looked like fog. The only reason she'd come to campus at all was because the plows were so lazy on weekends. If she were going to be holed up in her cottage for the next two days, she wanted to spend them with Mondrian, for the man was a genius with visual rhythms. She'd been sketching the Friday pub meetings lately, and wanted to try taking a non-figurative approach, capturing instead of the physical interactions themselves, those of the energy of the conflict and epiphany that she perceived to be underlying them.

But now leaving the library with her backpack full of art books, she was thinking only about the long walk home. Already the sidewalks were coated in white and the roads would have been treacherous on her bike. In her hurry she brushed the arm of a person coming up the stairs, and his own books tumbled down them.

One landed at her feet and with a murmured apology she bent and collected it. Rising again she took him in, crouching opposite her to gather the rest. For a moment she studied him, his furry head, his pale hands like paws, and the overall softness to him—all details that were familiar to her, and yet once again new.

Looking up then, his eyes widened, and his lips parted in surprise. Close-cropped hairs edged the thin lips like shards of gold, each one reflecting back at her the snow-light as he said, "Laurelie! I haven't seen you around since our philosophy class. I thought you'd graduated, actually."

She nodded. "I did. I'm in the MFA program now."

She brushed off the fresh dusting of snow that had accumulated on his book in the few minutes she'd had it in her hands and held it out to him. It was red-bound and gold-lettered with a plain dark cover. *Constructing Torts*, it said.

"Thanks. It's not a cookbook, you know," he said, and she watched a slow blush creep around his grin. "I'm doing my honor's thesis on the influence of linguistics on law."

The linguistic major switched to beer after one mug of cider, but she stayed with the warm fragrant drink, sipping it slowly and looking out the window as she listened to him pointing out linguistic loopholes in the Constitution. The light was fading now, and the snow was coming down fast. She imagined it was laying a great bandage upon the earth, under which it would become whole again, and new. A fire burned merrily in the fireplace, and she imagined Kvothe the wizard and Roland the gunslinger sitting before it with their heads together. *One broken,* Kvothe murmured, *and the other sick, so how could either heal? See how this one leans in,* Roland agreed, *how he pitches his voice so earnest and low. He wants to make her new.*

On the stage behind them, someone fingered a bass. A drum kicked, a flute rippled, and a fiddle trotted after it. Their tight, high-energy music spread through her and she closed her eyes, feeling the rhythm change and change and change again.

Jason had fallen silent. Opening her eyes, she found him holding his mouth like there was something in it and looking down at his bottle, turning it in his soft pale hands. Seeing the glass's slow revolution and the firelight reflected there, she wondered how gentle they would be.

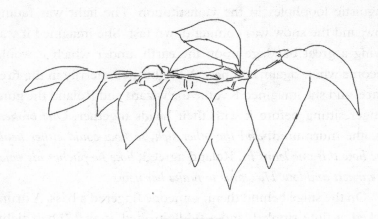

21

Laurelie reached up without looking away from her panels and grabbed the close-knit cardigan that had lived all winter on the arm of her couch. She stuffed her arms into its sleeves and returned to her work, but a few minutes later put down her colored pencils again and sighed. The extra sweater made five layers on her torso, and not only was she still cold, but her arm movement was now significantly compromised. For a moment a strong sensory memory of fur sliding over bare skin flooded her mind, before she pushed it away again.

She could have moved up to the couch from the floor. There was so little insulation in the cottage's walls that it was four degrees warmer up there; she'd actually measured the difference one day with a meat thermometer. But apart from the cold she had a perfect nest of pillows down on the floor, surrounded by her cats and her best heavy weight paper. She'd been down there ever since the snow started, the whole day slipping by while she worked.

Even after a few dozen snowstorms in this house, still the quiet surprised her. Storm was far too fierce a word, she thought, for what was going on out there. Beyond her picture window the world was white and round and still, nothing moving except the steadily falling snow. The flakes were fat and slow now though, which meant the storm would be ending soon. One would never know it but today was actually the first day of spring. There'd been hints of it in recent days, flashes of birdsong she wasn't sure she'd heard, a faint rotting smell she wasn't sure she'd smelled as the old snow crept back into the shadows, and yesterday the roads had been clear enough to bike to campus. Coming home again she'd noticed the river ice was turning yellow from the heating tannins in the water below.

But overnight winter had come roaring back. Rowan and Dark, at least, would be elated. Tomorrow she'd take them to scale the mountains left behind by the plows and skate the driveways where puddles had refrozen. Rowan would tell a tale as they went, of tracking monsters and giants by their footprints in the snow. He talked constantly now, a stream of consciousness that ran so fast sometimes all she could make out were the conjunctions, *an den, an den.* But still she grasped the images he painted, as if when something came from that deep inside an imagination, it didn't matter on what vehicle it was conveyed.

Looking down at her panels, she wondered if the same could be said about them. She was working on a new series, one that scared her a little, and sometimes a lot, for it involved completely regular people doing completely regular things, and moreover not at all painfully. She was using techniques derived from Vermeer and Morandi, who had also painted the things one saw every day, but so luminously as to capture something deeply essential, something magical about them. The panels before her now showed a student simply walking down an empty hallway. The person was slender and nondescript, wearing khaki slacks and a pale blue oxford and brown shoes, carrying a musical instrument in a small black case. Smooth brown hair lay close against the scalp and the face and eyes were bare of expression, as if lost in thought. The thought bubbles rising from the chest and head contained only notes of music. She was trying, as the panels focused in, to use light and shape to make the face grow more rapturous, and at the same time make the music in the thought bubbles more complex, building in the penultimate panel to a feeling she wanted to seem almost like desire as the face filled it completely, all skin and eyes and lips. Then in the final panel the form was shown from behind, again genderless and nondescript, but for a sleek brown ponytail that swayed long and sinuously to the waist.

But it was so hard to make something feel magical without the props of fantasy, and moreover her fingers had stiffened now from the cold. She decided to warm them around a cup of hot chocolate. Maybe she'd even light a fire. Will was usually the fire builder, but it would be another hour before he and Scottie arrived, if they even made it at all in this weather. Though they'd never missed a Saturday yet, always showing up at sunset with takeout and a movie and then hanging out in her living room feeding the fire and talking until long after midnight. Scottie called it camping.

She smiled. A fire would be perfect. But seeing the basket beside her fireplace empty gave her pause. If she wanted a fire, she was going to have to go for logs. She decided it was worth it. After putting on her snow boots, parka, hat and gloves, she pulled open the front door only to find a waist-high snow drift blocking her way. She clambered around it, sinking deep enough even at the sides that snow went down her boots, and imagined winter chuckling gleefully. Now she headed for the porch stairs, proceeding down them much more cautiously, for a foot of fresh snow lay upon them and she knew from past experience that black ice might be hiding underneath. However, the late season snow was heavy and sticky, and this gave her traction as she descended. It also made traversing the leaden drifts hard work and she soon grew hot, plunging her way around the house to the eaves at the back.

Finally, the woodpile. One column remained, stacked high and tight; the rest Will had been steadily gnawing away at all winter. She studied the column while she caught her breath, and soon discerned a pattern. It was planned well, shards and broken pieces tucked in so that both logs and kindling could be gathered in a single armful. Clutching one, she started back. The going was easier now, following her own footsteps. In the quiet she heard nothing but the crunch of her own boots and the beat of her own heart, perceiving the great and singular whiteness like a presence, or rather an absence, a void. Nothing else was alive on the surface, but many were lying in cold torpor beneath it, waiting for the sun to awaken them. But already the pale light was retreating, and the touch of the wind promised another cold night.

Inside her cottage she clumped directly to the fireplace and dumped her load in the basket. Her cats woke then and grew playful, stalking the white geometric tracks she'd left across the floor while she built her fire. She took her time with it, weaving a large loose bed of paper twists and kindling and then erecting above it a magnificent teepee of logs. The result so pleased her that she lingered a little while after lighting it, watching the flames consume the paper and lick up the sides of the wood.

In the kitchen she filled a pan with milk and added half a bar of chocolate. She stirred until it began to steam and then, smelling smoke, remembered her fire and headed back to the living room to check on it.

Halfway there she halted in shock. Fat white ribbons spiraled lazily out of the fireplace, slowly diffusing into a room already hung with clouds of smoke. Running to the front door she threw it wide, and then ran back to the kitchen and opened the window there too. Tugging at drawers, she looked for something she could use to push up the flue, for she'd been so focused on making her fire that she'd forgotten to open it.

Grabbing a wooden spoon and dishtowel, she hurried back toward the living room. But hardly had she stepped into the front hall when she heard footsteps on the porch. Moments later two forms burst in. Both black, the first one was so large it took the snowdrift without losing a step. The other one sailed like a shadow right over it. And then, still trailing swirls of white, both of them disappeared into the smoke seeping from her living room.

She followed them, uncertain what she'd seen, half-believing that in her alarm she'd imagined it. Then upon entering the smoke she forgot everything else, for her eyes began to sting and her lungs burned and she began to cough forcefully, unable to take a single clean breath. She covered her nose and mouth with the dishtowel and breathed shallowly through it, but it hardly helped. Unable to see and blinded by tears, she simply continued on until she felt heat, and then suddenly the fireplace was before her, still seething angry fat billows of white, and a man was crouched on the hearth before it.

For it was a man. The treads of his black boots were still clotted with snow. His face was tucked deep into the collar of his black coat, and his black watch cap was pulled down low. Behind him paced a black dog, whining and pawing at his legs. Already the man was reaching into the fire. For a long moment his arm hung there while snakes of flame writhed hungrily beneath it and tried to reach it by scaling the tepee of logs. Then finally there came a squeaky creak, and the arm was snatched out again.

The hiker stood on the porch taking deep slow breaths of the cold pinkening air, while she stood in the doorway taking quick shallow ones, feeling each one like a tiny icy fingernail scraping her stinging lungs.

She looked at the two prints he'd left in the snowdrift, one coming in and another going out again. But for them he could have been the specter of her long imaginings. In the dusky light his eyes were wide obsidian brushstrokes, his lips a crimson slash. His features looked cut from marble and the tracks his blood took were clearly visible beneath skin gone sallow after so many months without sun.

In his long coat he appeared larger than she remembered, not only taller but broader as well. It wasn't black as she'd first thought, but rather a dark brown fur-lined leather, with a trail of darker stain marring the arm he'd placed in the path of the flames. From that hand now he slowly removed his glove. His movements were careful as he opened and closed his fingers, but she thought the skin did not look burned, and after a minute he seemed to agree, for he put the glove back on.

But his gaze stayed down, and again came the feeling that the scene before her wasn't real. And the longer it went without him looking at her, the more heightened the sensation grew. *How odd*, she thought after a while, *if he really is here, and the only thing I am wondering is why.*

The dog finally moved, breaking the spell. Trotting down off the porch, he leapt around her yard lapping at the deep snow.

"Sorry," the hiker murmured now. "I didn't mean to intrude. I—I smelled paint burning."

"But . . ." Even as she shook her head, she was following his tracks in the snow, back through her yard and across the lane to where they disappeared down the river trail. "But she's not there. You took her."

Leather whispered as he shifted. "She wouldn't go."

Her throat was dry. And his must have been too for he followed her inside, telling her quietly about the bob-kittens, how big they'd grown even if they didn't act it yet. Hearing his pride, she found herself picturing—still in his cabin clearing, the idea persisting despite what he'd said—him cuffing the young bobcats gently and wrestling with them, as a big brother would. The image was so clear; it was the one before her now that was still so hazy, so undefined. He looked like an old photograph of himself, one taken from far away. She handed him a mug of water and then felt time warp and shift as he upended it and drank it all in one long series of swallows.

"Sorry. I don't have any alcohol," she said.

"That's okay. I don't want any. But a little of that would be nice. I've been out in the cold a while."

She turned then, surprised to find her pot of hot chocolate still steaming on the stove. Taking his mug, she poured him some and then handed it back again. She poured the rest into a mug for herself, only to find that, lips on cup, she couldn't sip. Instead she stared out the window at a child's drawing of winter, and imagined the bobcat prowling across the snow with silent feet. Not safe in his woods, but rather out there all along. The bobcat had stayed in the world with her, after all.

The hiker had moved into her line of sight and was gently rubbing the leaf of one of the potted plants on the counter by the window. Angered by the sight of their long dead trailing stalks, she'd cut them down one fall afternoon. A week later, after a brief warm spell, she'd been shocked to see they'd sprouted new baby leaves. By now the stalks trailed again down the sides of the pots, and though without summer's light they hadn't flowered, still his touch released the sweet perfume of tomatoes.

"You brought them inside," he said, and his voice was low and vital, like the one that still murmured in her dreams. "Fruit's even better the second year."

She flushed then, grew hot. "I should check the fire," she said.

Hurrying then, birdlike, through the hall, she was relieved to find that with the front door open most of the smoke had cleared. But why was the living room so dark? It took a moment for her eyes to process the fact that what she was seeing was the wall. The entire area above the fireplace looked like it had been splattered with tar. The sticky mass streaked upward from the mantle, thinning away at both sides into charred and bubbling paint. The shocking sight was only made worse by the healthy fire now crackling beneath it, its flames not writhing hungrily, but stretching straight and tall.

The hiker moved past her. He had removed his coat, and he held it in one hand as he went close to the wall, and with his ear to it slowly and methodically knocked up and down the whole burned width with his knuckles. There was no structural damage, he told her, wiping his knuckles on his jeans, leaving a long black streak. The wall would need to be scraped and repainted, but it was half a day's work, no more.

She nodded, focused on the thick gray fisherman's sweater he wore. She'd never seen it before, but from its rolled collar she caught a glimpse of a familiar hollow and two round bones. His hair was shorter, the commas escaping from his cap so blue-black they made a black hat look gray.

If he felt her watching he gave no sign—and it was on this detail rather than the others that her mind suddenly fixed. For even from as far back as she stood, the reek of the charred wall was strong, but his nose wasn't flared, or even flickering. His mouth was closed and his eyes were dry. His face was still.

Now he turned away from her and slipped the poker from its stand. He prodded the fire and her teepee disintegrated, sending sparks and black feathers floating down onto logs already embedded deep with chunks of glowing embers. They regarded these in silence for a time before he put back the poker and turned back to face her.

Slowly then, he raised the sleeve of his sweater. "A couple of months ago," he said, "I cut my arm."

She saw it immediately, the thin pink puckered line, perfectly straight as it crossed a stretch of limb she remembered as smooth and dark. He'd been working late one night at his cabin, he told her as he pulled the sleeve down again, cutting a plank of pine for a windowsill. His table saw had caught a knot and flipped the plank back at him. There'd been so much blood that he'd decided he needed stitches, and so he'd wrapped it up and driven to his parents' house.

He bent then and took a log from the basket and laid it on the fire. Crouching there, he watched the fire take it with a coiled intensity that made Laurelie see double, and told her how his mother had sewn his arm up again. But he'd smelled her fear while she did it, he said. Not from the cut, which was long but shallow enough. She'd been so careful about cleaning up, he said, that she must have been afraid of all the blood.

Back at his cabin there was even more of it. His fingerprints were on almost every surface and he'd tracked it all over the floor as well. It had spattered on the wall behind the saw and dripped all over the pile of wood he'd been cutting. It had looked like a murder scene, he said. And standing there taking it in he'd thought about his mother, how she skinned deer and beheaded birds without any qualms. She wouldn't have been afraid just by the sight of his blood. She'd been afraid of what was inside it.

He'd started cleaning then, he said, and had kept on cleaning long after he could no longer see his blood, because he could still smell it. Eventually, exhausted, he'd had to stop and face the fact that he'd never get it all. Some of it had already been absorbed into the walls and floor and was now part of the cabin itself.

"Not safe at all," he murmured. "Contaminated."

He began pulling small bits of kindling from the basket now and feeding them to the flames. He told her he'd called the CDC and left a message with a receptionist. She'd thought he was crazy, but Dr. Waters had called him back the very next day.

They'd met at the Portland Medical Center, a few hours' drive away. The hospital had a CDC-affiliated lab and Waters had been able to arrange lab access. The hiker had told the doctor he wouldn't last even a day; the bright lights and loud machines and smells of sickness made it, for him, a torture chamber. But Dr. Waters had told him that these reactions would be good, that the tests would be more accurate if his symptoms were exacerbated. So they'd agreed that he could camp in the woods next to the hospital, and come to the lab only for as long as he could stand it each day.

In the weeks that followed Waters had run every test he knew on the hiker's blood, and all his other body fluids besides. He'd been given neurological and physical exams, and a whole battery of sensory and reaction time tests. Eventually Dr. Waters had even started making up his own tests. Once, the hiker said, he'd had to distinguish a hundred different scents transmitted inside a vapor simultaneously, but that actually hadn't been as difficult as it sounded, because most of them had been culinary or botanical.

Peeling back a thick hunk of bark, the hiker said that all the testing had an unanticipated effect—it had helped him learn control. He could spend whole days at the lab now, and hardly react at all. He still slept at his camp, but that was less for physical reasons than mental ones now. It still felt like home, he said. There was a family of deer that slept nearby, and late at night a red fox stole through. A fisher cat screamed sometimes like a nightmare, and some mornings he found signs of black bear.

Now his voice changed. In a monotone, he said, "No signs of active virus to date," and because he was staring at the piece of bark, it seemed as if it were a phrase he were reading there. All his senses measured beyond the ninety-ninth human percentile, he said, so they had to compare him to animals. He smelled as well as a dog, he said, and saw like an owl, and heard like a hawk. He tasted as well as a catfish, and his touch was a sensitive as a mole's. But they still didn't know how his brain processed the extra data, or how it affected his consciousness.

He fell silent then, and for a moment she was sure his nostrils flickered. Outlined in fire, the black of his eyes went liquid as he stared into its flickering light, and this made him appear almost otherworldly. And yet after all, he was only a man. He was no Joan of Arc either, for his internal experiences had physical correlates. The stimuli his brain responded to existed outside of his head. It was as if someone had picked up her world and shaken all the pieces loose, and yet the strongest thing Laurelie felt was relief for him.

She listened to the flames. To her they made a burring, rushing sound not unlike the wind. She was certain however that it sounded different to him, and equally certain she'd never know exactly how. For no matter how close two physical bodies came they never became one. Even connected they remained separate, and responsible first to themselves, and even in love they made no whole but rather two halves of a deeply flawed, almost perfect thing. She pictured this thing, sketched it first and then put it into the fire and heated it, and held it to her mind until it branded deep.

The hiker was threading the piece of bark through his fingers like a magician's coin, telling her how Waters had deduced that the virus must have moved through his blood, for this was the only possible explanation of how the sensory receptor replication had occurred over so much of his body. And while there were no longer active virus particles in his blood, no one knew if any were hiding dormant elsewhere. And they wouldn't ever know unless the virus reactivated so that they could trace its path. That's why his blood would be tested for the rest of his life. To make sure he didn't infect anyone else.

She moved then, and the bark that had been whirling in his fingers froze, poised there like wings. She could surprise him still, it seemed. The room was dark but for the fire, and so she snapped on the lamp as she walked to the picture window. She pressed her forehead to the icy window glass and felt winter's cold breath slipping through the ancient frame. But the darkness outside was impenetrable, reflecting back only the room behind her.

"What if someone didn't mind?" She spoke so softly her breath left no mist, but she saw the bark fall from his hands. The room was so quiet she heard it land. Infected then with what her question had woken, another ancient sickness for which there was no cure. There was only the hiker coming toward her full of his animal grace, his nostrils wide to smell her, his mouth open to taste her, his hands flexing at his sides to touch her even as he came. She turned then and gloried in the meeting of their gazes, the pull so strong it felt like falling.

Someone tapped out *Shave and a Haircut* on the front door.

"Um. Hello? Lars? There's a strange dog wandering around outside. And by the way, why is your door open?"

Laughter then, followed by scuffling and scraping sounds.

"There's a small mountain blocking our way as well, but never mind. We've cleared a path," Scottie said.

"I think I may have pulled a muscle, actually," said Will.

And then Laurelie's friends tumbled through the door. They

removed their gloves and boots and coats and hats in a snowy flurry of limbs and stacked them around the radiator with a carelessness that bespoke of familiarity.

Turning toward the living room then Will stopped short, so that Scottie bumped into him. Neither spoke, but they leaned together, taking her in, along with the man next to her. And for a moment, she saw through their eyes, the two faces with their fixed expressions, the contrast of their bodies, one larger and darker, the other smaller and lighter. She felt the hiker sway beside her then; it was almost infinitesimal, the barest brush of his body against hers, as if she had by some strange gravity drawn him in. She felt this even through five layers of clothing, and energy surged outward from her core toward him, silent and fecund, and when it reached her skin she looked up at him, and he looked down at her, and his nostrils flickered, just once.

"Um, so this is Lucien," she said then, turning and looking at her friends. "And this is Scottie. And this is Will."

"'Allo," said Scottie. Smiling as he bounced a little on the balls of his feet.

"Hello," said Will. His own expression was mostly hidden by his beard.

Lucien blinked a few times rapidly. His nose wrinkled and his nostrils flared, and then suddenly he turned around and bent down. When he rose again the little girl cat was in his arms, her claws piercing the fabric of his jacket with tiny popping sounds. He stroked the bristles beneath her chin, and in the silence they all heard the crackle in her throat as she began to purr.

"Nice to meet you," he said, looking up, and smiled.

ACKNOWLEDGMENTS

Thank you first and foremost to Pamela Malpas of the Jennifer Lyons Literary Agency, for seeing potential in *The Bobcat* and not letting it rest. My many thanks and admiration also to the wonderful Lilly Golden, my editor at Arcade, who lives in the woods too and made a perfect match for *The Bobcat*. Thank you as well to Emily Labes, Johanna Dickson, and the rest of the team at Arcade/Skyhorse for seeing us through to publication.

My eternal gratitude goes to the writers Jack Livings and Jennie Yabroff. "We're all in this together," they told me, and I've come to see it's true. I'm also unspeakably grateful to the DebutAuthors'19 FB group for their camaraderie and insights during the year and more preceding our respective publications. Also, much appreciation goes to Ken and Christie Gordon and Andrew Miles, who for no benefit of their own took the time to help *The Bobcat* find its audience. I'm also grateful to my fellow travelers at the American Academy in Rome, where *The Bobcat* was finished; quietly under the Roman pines we supported each other's good work (and seriously barbecued).

Thanks to my pre-pub readers for their encouragement and/or criticism, including Zack Finch, Kelley Hersey, Mary Plourde, Myrna Gabbe, Elaine Sirkin Forbes and her entire book group, Sarah Fineman, Patricia Keating, Diane Blandino.

Love and gratitude to my Bermudian father, Chris Forbes, for encouraging my first stories and teaching me romantic poetry, and to my Jamaican mother-in-law, Beryl Walters Riley, whose intelligence and beauty have long inspired me.

Forever and always to Enrico, whose sensitivity never ceases to surprise me, and Alexander and Etienne, those strange and beautiful creatures we produced.